MW01134063

1

Also by Thomas Muller

Four Corners

No More Tales to Tell

Catherine

Catherine

Catherine

Thomas Muller

Thoughts from the author

I composed the first draft of this story in 2010, only without an ending. The story itself ended abruptly, mid-sentence, waiting for me to return. A few years later, I met Eugene Mont while working at Keuka College. He and I, along with many others on staff and some of the students, collaborated to create a few interesting fan films and have good times.

The writing involved in those led to a proposal for a full-length project – a horror film – that sadly didn't get made due to lack of time. But out of that process, Eugene and I continued to write, even after he left Keuka. After a joint venture on which we both tackled story and extra elements, and picking up representation in Hollywood, we each started our own solo projects for film and TV. Eugene's first attempt was a screenplay called *The Diary*, a story to this day I demand must be made, as I have both read and edited it, and feel it is akin to *Silence of the Lambs* for this generation.

My first solo project was my baby, Catherine. My decision to take what was a short novel and adapt it for the screen seemed daunting at first. Going from book to screen, you tend to lose a lot, and just about everyone I know who has read a book and watched the subsequent film, prefer the former every single time.

And this also meant that I would have to give the story an ending.

The writing, at first, was a long process. I tried like hell to adhere to as much of the story that I could. When it was done, and edited multiple times, Eugene and I began querying agents all throughout Los Angeles. One day, while at work, my cell phone rang. I glanced at the number, didn't recognize it, and went back to work. But then the phone chimed, and I had a new voicemail.

It was an agent. From Los Angeles. And he was interested, and wanted to talk.

Excitement! How the hell does someone in upstate New York get attention from someone in the industry? I called Eugene quickly, then I called the agent. We talked for twenty minutes, and he requested the script. I was on my way!

Sadly, those who know the business know how difficult this process can be. Within weeks, *Catherine* had garnered no interest, and the agent was more interested in another project of ours, *Demon* (a damn fine story if there ever was one).

However, all of our shots missed the mark during this tenure, and we parted ways with the agent. And *Catherine* languished on the shelf, forgotten for many years.

When I went to publish my first book last year, it came down to *Catherine* or *Four Corners*, of which the latter won. Okay, second book…nah.

This was tough. Of all the characters I've created, Sheriff Will is one that I love the most. I've had many conversations over the years with people about stories and characters, and he's one of the first ones I either mention, or at least, comes to mind.

That's sad to me, for I spent years writing solo projects and working with Eugene on many joint projects as well. All together, we have (if my math is correct) 13 full length projects, four short film scripts, five short films actually produced, numerous short stories, and the outline for a book series.

And Will always came back into my mind.

So, this is the right time. It's Will's moment in the spotlight, whatever that may be. I'm hoping that this exercise treats him well.

For those of you who have stuck with me through these three books, I thank you. It means a lot to someone who just likes to tell stories.

To those of you who are new, I hope you enjoy a little trip to the Town of Catherine.

Dedicated to my father, Tom.

1

A car swerved back and forth along the icy country road, fishtailed, and tore through the snow-covered field at a high rate of speed. Somewhat deep with at least six inches already on the ground with a heavy snow falling, the car left a nasty divot in the snow as it gained speed, vaulting down the field toward a patch of pine trees. The driver did not attempt to turn or brake.

It came to a sudden, jolting halt after connecting with a large pine tree. The branches of that tree and a few surrounding trees shook as the snow continued to blanket the scene, shrouding the car and the pines.

2

A 1999 Ford Taurus police car carefully traversed through the wind-blown snow. Sheriff Will Putner sighed and looked at the dashboard clock; 9:14.

He pulled his squad car onto the shoulder, parking behind a tractor with a plow on the front. His gloved hand grabbed the door handle and pushed with his leg at the same time, and the door squeaked open with some effort. Will tugged his winter hat over his greying hair and ears, stepped from the car, and zipped his winter coat all the way up to his chin. He sucked in a breath - a sharp inhale of harsh winter air - and coughed.

"Will!"

Will glanced down to the edge of the field and noticed Daryl Watson shrouded in the blowing snow.

Daryl was a round, baby-faced man wearing a plaid snow suit.

"Hey Will, how are ya? How's the bronchitis?" Daryl hollered as he walked towards the cop.

"Good."

Daryl approached Will, stomping his boots on the ground to knock off some crusty snow.

"Good to see ya make it out. Wasn't sure if you'd make it up here."

"Where's it at?" Will asked as he looked down into the field.

Daryl's face was beet-like, both in roundness and in color.   He turned awkwardly, shifting his torso before moving his feet, and pointed down the field.

"Okay, get right to it, eh," he said, his breath labored, "well, it's right down there, behind that first patch of pine into the second."

As the pair made their way down the field, Will turned and glanced back at his car.

"Quite a ways down. How'd you find it?"

"I was heading up to Mabel's to move snow away from the barn. Mother-in-laws, right?" Daryl chuckled at his own little joke. "Anyway, as I come up the road here, I noticed somethin' shining from down here."

"You saw it through the fog?"

"Fog was gone when I got down here."

"Must be over a couple hundred feet from the road..."

"Yep," Daryl replied heavily as he tried to keep up with the sheriff. To their left was a small patch of pine trees. They passed them and came to a larger clump of pine. The outer limbs of the trees sagged under the weight of the wet snow. Between two very large pine trees, the bumper of a car jutted out, slightly tilted to the left. Will reached down with a gloved hand and brushed snow away from the license plate.

"Oh, good thinkin'…" Daryl said as he watched Will crouch next to the plate. Will took out a notepad and a pen from his coat pocket and scratched down the plate number. He then moved slowly through the deep snow and under one of the tree limbs to the passenger side of the car. Using his feet, he kicked snow away from the passenger side door.

"This door ain't shut..." Will spoke. Daryl eyes sprung wide open with thrilled anticipation.

"Maybe it come open in the wreck." The cold did not dampen Daryl's interest as he stood just beyond Will's shoulder, watching intently.

"Maybe..."

Will tugged on the door, plowing the remainder of the snow around it, until the door swung open. He leaned over slowly and exhaled as he poked his head inside the car.

"Anything?" Daryl asked excitedly.

"Yep." Will reached across the seat and nudged the body sitting slumped behind the steering wheel, resting against the driver's side door, its face black and purple, and covered with frost. The body of the man was wearing a light jacket over a tee-shirt along with blue jeans and sneakers.

"He's been here a while."

"Who?"

"The driver," Will replied.

"He dead?"

Will tapped the side of the dead man's head. "Frozen solid."

"We could thaw him out."

Will leaned out of the car. "Don't think that will help him."

3

The tow truck arrived, parked behind a red truck that was behind Will's car, and a thin wisp of a man climbed out of the cab. The faded red logo on the side of the truck read Scooter's Garage, and as Scooter slammed the driver's door, he ran his gloved-hand over his name.

Daryl had driven his tractor back to his farm, grabbed two shovels and a come-along, and returned to the scene in his pickup truck. He and Will were digging out the car as Scooter stepped to the side of the road and waved.

"Hey!"

Will looked up at Scooter, then over to Daryl, who was huffing pretty heavily. "What time is it?"

Daryl peeled up his coat sleeve and looked at his digital watch.

"Ten after ten."

"We best get moving, then," Will replied. Scooter noticed Daryl hooking his come-along to the car, and Scooter jumped back into his truck and maneuvered it so that the winch was angled to the field. Daryl and Will inched the car out from under the second patch of pines, with the come-along strung to a tree, little by little, until they were near the first group of trees. Once there, Scooter released his cable and trudged his way into the field to meet the sheriff and the farmer. It was nearly noon when the tan Toyota was hauled up to the road.

Scooter noticed the body behind the wheel and shuddered.

"Don't you want to call EMS and get him outta here?"

"Can't help him," Will said through frozen lips, "I'll call county when we get back to town."

Scooter led the two-mile procession back into town followed by Will, who was followed by Daryl. They pulled into the lot at Scooter's garage and parked behind the building, which was in good shape except for the faded blue paint job.

Scooter lowered the car to the ground.

"So, Sheriff, what do you think happened?

Will walked around the car, inspecting it as he went.

"Probably going a little too fast late at night on a road he didn't know and lost control."

"Accident or foul play, Will?"

Will stopped and glanced at Daryl. There was absolute joy in his question. Even though it were March, Daryl was sweating.

"It was an accident, Daryl." Will resumed his walk around the car. "Well, there's damage to both front quarter panels as well as massive damage to the front end. I bet the undercarriage sustained serious damage as well."

Scooter dropped to the ground and slid his slender body under the car near the front passenger tire.

"Got a broken rod," he said, his voice somewhat muffled, "oh, and it looks like the oil pan's shredded."

"Good enough, Scooter." Will's affirmation brought Scooter back to his feet. Will stopped walking as he got to the driver's side door.

"I'm gonna head over to the office, make a few calls, and do a little paperwork. Can you two do me a favor?"

"Sure!" Daryl exclaimed as Scooter nodded.

"Stay here and watch the car. Go in Scooter's garage and stay warm. Have a coffee. Just don't let anyone near this car until I get back."

4

Will unlocks the door to the Town of Catherine Sheriff's Office and steps inside. The office is a cramped space with a large wooden desk to the right of the door, two three-drawer filing cabinets behind it against the wall, his desk chair, a small press board bookcase with binders tipped and tossed all over it, three wooden chairs facing the desk, and, to the left, two holding cells. There are two doors at the back of the room - one is a closet for storage and the other a small bathroom with only a toilet and sink.

Without removing his coat, Will sat at his desk, picked up his phone, and punched the number pad.

"Buck...Will Putner..."

"Will, how the hell are ya," Buck replied in an overly loud voice, "this ain't another bovine call, is it?

"I'm doing alright...and, yeah, I remember the Holstein..."

"Yeah, sure as hell was..."

"Yeah, hey Buck, this ain't a social call," Will interrupted, "I got business, a one car accident. One DB, no hurry. Ain't nothing changing."

There was a short pause, as if this information was being considered.

"Well, dammit Will, you caught me at the right time. I'll be up. Meet you at your office?"

"Scooter's Garage," Will replied.

"On my way."

Will dropped the receiver on its base. He pulled the whole phone unit closer to him and sat back in his chair. He picked up the phone and punched in more numbers.

"County Sheriff's Office, this is Jeannie speaking. How may I direct your call?"

"Hey Jeannie, this is Sheriff Will Putner, Town of Catherine. I'm calling in a one vehicle MVA."

"Hi, Will. Long time...you need emergency services?"

"Nah, I called Buck."

"Oh, the driver's deceased," Jeannie said as she typed on her end, "anyone else in the vehicle?"

"Nope, just one deceased male," Will answered, then paused, "hey, Jeannie, let David know I called, would you? Thanks a lot."

Will dropped the receiver back on the cradle before Jeannie could respond, and stared at it. He went to reach for the phone again then paused, pulling his hand back slowly.

5

Will stepped inside the office at Scooter's Garage. The office was dirty and grimy, with grease and dust caked over pretty much everything in there. There was a counter that ran the length of the small room with a three-foot space between the cabinet and the wall closest to the garage, giving access behind the counter. The back wall was littered with road signs, license plates, and product signs. To the right, there was a door that led to the two-bay garage. To the left, the office contains an empty old shelf, a couch stained with oil and grease, and a stack of used tires. The room itself had a strong odor of motor oil, which turned Will's stomach a bit.

Scooter was behind the counter. He reached below the countertop and retrieved a coffee pot. He poured the coffee into a spot-riddled cup, walked around, and handed it to Will. The sheriff tipped the cup and looked at it carefully before putting it to his lips. Scooter walked back and leaned on the counter. Daryl had pulled two tires out onto the floor and was using them as a seat instead of the couch.

Will remained standing in the doorway as Daryl and Scooter continued the conversation he walked in on.

"I bet a white-tail bolted out in front of him and he swerved and lost control," Scooter theorized.

Daryl slowly nodded in agreement, then paused.

"Could've happened...or, maybe, he had a few too many and drove right off the road. Had to be going pretty fast - you see how far off the road he was?"

"Yep..." Scooter considered.

"What about you, Will," Daryl said as he turned to the man responsible for their conspiracy theories, "what do you think?"

"Find out soon enough."

Will turned his stare out the door as Scooter and Daryl continued to drone on, which Will was able to tune out.

Nearly twenty minutes later, a 1983 Chevy Pickup pulled into the parking lot at Scooter's Garage, followed by an ambulance. The dark blue truck came to a sudden stop right outside the door that Will occupied as the ambulance slowed to a stop at the entrance of the lot.

A short, fit man with a cleanly shaven head emerged from the truck and hurried over to Will, who had stepped out from the doorway. Buck extended his hand, and Will took it.

"Hey, Will, how the hell are ya?"

"Whistlin' cold..."

"Yeah, I hear that," Buck chuckled, "it's been a long time. Keeping busy out here in the boonies?"

"Here and there, Buck."

"That's good, that's good," Buck said, beaming as he looked at his old friend. "You look good for an old fart."

"You're a few years older than me, you ornery old bastard."

Buck started laughing and slapped Will on the arm.

"Hell, you know I turn the big five-o next month, eh?"

Will cracked a slight smile. "Senior citizen. At least you'll get a discount on your coffee."

"Fuck you," Buck replied, and they both laughed. After a moment, Buck looked around. "Say, what've you got?"

Will pointed towards the back of the garage.

"It's out back."

Will set the coffee cup on the ground as he and Buck started walking.

"Male Caucasian, probably mid-to-late twenties," Will continued, "wait til you see this."

The pair rounded the corner of the building and the wrecked car sat in front of them. Will held up a hand to Buck, which caused the latter to stop next to the car. Will crossed to the passenger side and slid in the seat. He took a firm hold of the body.

"Ok...open the driver's door."

Buck opened the door. The frozen body slid slightly out of the door but Will kept a firm grip.

"Whoa, are you kidding me," Buck said, shocked, "this fella's frozen solid!"

Buck dropped to one knee, ran his hand over the dead man's skull, and whistled. Will maintained his grip on the dead man's arm, holding him in position while Buck surveyed the damage.

"Well, he has obvious trauma to the head," Buck reported, "probably bounced off everything within range of his seat." He paused. "But I'll know more when I get him on the table."

"Keep this in county," Will said quietly, "I don't want this going state."

"Okay," Buck said as he glanced up at his friend.

Will's hand begins cramping. "You got all you need in here?"

"Yep. Let's get him out."

Buck turned and motioned for the ambulance. The emergency transport efficiently backed up to the car. A young driver got out, opened the back of the wagon, and pulled out a gurney.

"I got 'em," Buck said as he braced the dead body with his shoulder. Will released his grip and slid out of the car. He walked around to the driver's side.

"Where's your rig," Will asked as stopped behind the coroner.

"In the shop," Buck chuckled as he shook his head, "transmission. Soaking me for over two grand. Can you believe that? Actually, soaking the county... so it ain't my money. Til I get it back, I get to use a county ambulance. Nice, huh?"

Will smiled politely and nodded as the paramedic wheeled the gurney over to the pair. Will and the driver each grabbed the body while Buck got up. He brushed snow and dirt off his pants, and then the three tipped the body until it was almost onto the gurney.

They picked up the body and centered it is as best they could. Once it is strapped down, the gurney was lifted into the back of the ambulance. The driver shut the rear doors, gave Will a friendly nod, and disappeared back to the driver's seat of the ambulance.

Will noticed Daryl and Scooter standing at the corner of the garage, watching as the events unfolded.

"Hey, listen, I'll do a prelim when I get back," Buck spoke, snapping Will's concentration, "and don't worry, it looks like an accident so it won't have to go state."

"I appreciate that."

Buck watched Will for a moment. "Still no love lost?" Will did not answer, instead, he looked off into the distance. Buck waited, then continued, "I see...ok, I'll call you when I know anything."

The ambulance followed Buck's pickup off the lot as Will walked back to the wrecked car.

6

Will pulled his Sheriff's car into his driveway on Felton Road and glanced at the clock on the radio. 5:20.

He parked outside the second bay of the attached two car garage and shuffled around the garage to the back door of the large two-story house. He entered the house through the kitchen door. The house is quiet.

Will crossed the kitchen to a picture-lined hallway, proceeded to the first door on his right and entered. His office was a drab space with faded walls and a dirt-matted carpet. Two of the walls were wood paneling and the other two were painted a dull tan. Dotting the walls were pictures - mostly of him in uniform - and two plaques. The plaques were old - one was the Governor's Merit Award for Bravery and the other was a completion certificate from the Police Academy.

Will removed his gun and placed it in the top drawer of his desk. With daylight waning through his lone office window, he stared out into his backyard for a moment, then walked out into the hall and past pictures of his family - his wife Teri, and his stepdaughter, Amy. It wasn't until he reached the bedroom to change that he found Ted, his nine-year-old Golden Retriever, stretched out and drooling on the bed.

Will changed into a sweatshirt and jeans without waking the dog.

Satisfied that the house was calm, he exited through the kitchen door and crossed the back yard to a small outbuilding that matched the look of his home, his shop.

7

Will looked at a wooden framed clock hanging on the wall.

7:30.

He had gotten hungry and ordered a Pizza from Mario's in town. They normally only deliver on weekends but, for the Sheriff, they made an exception. Will grabbed a slice from the box and stared at the work ahead of him as he chewed.

On his work bench in the center of the room was a medium sized cabinet and various tools. Along the back wall was a section of pegboard with various tools hanging on it, a small table, and a large cabinet that was open. Inside the cabinet were various tools in the bottom, a twelve-gauge shotgun that stood on top of a black duffel bag, and a top shelf that consisted of both small tools and shotgun shells.

Will took one last bite of the pizza and dropped the crust into the box. As he chewed, he snatched up a piece of sandpaper and walked over to the cabinet. He ran his hand over one edge slowly and stopped in a spot. He then carefully, deliberately ran the sandpaper over the edge.

Behind him, the door to the shop opened.

Without turning around, Will spoke.

"Where have you been?"

"I took Amy up to Arnot Mall," Teri replied with a touch of attitude, "she needed a new outfit. The soccer team has an away game at Athens this week."

Will put down the sandpaper and grabbed a palm sander.

"Did you eat?" Teri asked. Will pointed in the direction of the pizza box. Teri rolled her eyes, which made her look much older than the 37 years she was. "I'm going in the house."

Will gripped the power sander firmly and responded as she closed the door behind her.

"I'll be in shortly…"

8

Will entered the dark and quiet house just after ten-thirty that night, the lighted clock on the microwave beaming at him as closed the door.

He walked to the bathroom, brushed his teeth, then walked to the bedroom. Teri was asleep facing away from his side of the bed. Ted was stretched out on Will's side. Rather than move the dog, Will wandered to the living room and stretched out on the couch.

9

The town of Catherine was once a quaint little hamlet on the edge of Bradford County, but change in the economic structure imposed a minor exodus of its inhabitants elsewhere. There remained a few shops along the Main Street storefront and along a row of side streets. The gazebo in the center of town had boards missing from along the railing, and was in bad need of paint as well as repair.

Will turned from Main onto Cherry Street and parked his car in the spot marked SHERIFF. He stepped from his car and walked past his office, which was between Al's Hardware and the Catherine Diner.

Will entered the eatery and walked to the counter. The diner, set up like an old box car, had a row of windows along the front and a booth under each window. Opposite them was a long counter with metal stools bolted to the floor.

Tina, an older woman with bleach blonde hair that's pulled up in a ponytail, approached Will with a smile on her face. She carried a large Styrofoam cup.

"Hey, honey, anything special today?"

Will smiled at the waitress.

"English muffin with bacon."

She jotted the order down on a small pad then tapped her pen on the counter.

"How's Teri doin'?"

Will looked Tina in the eyes then looked around the diner.

"She's okay…good."

Tina smiled. "Tell her to stop in sometime. I haven't seen her in weeks."

"I'll do that," Will replied without looking at her.

Tina snapped the pen on the pad one last time, smiled, and took the order back to the cook, who acted quite busy. Will watched him for a moment, then scanned the restaurant.

Mr. Turner, the retired Social Studies teacher, sat at the far end of the counter hunched over a plate of scrambled eggs. Betsy Norfolk and Ann McKelvie sat in a booth near the door, chatting away. At the booth at the end of the row was a young couple that Will did not recognize.

"Here ya go, Sheriff," Tina said, startling Will. His breakfast was neatly wrapped in aluminum foil.

Will dropped a ten on the counter, grabbed the coffee and sandwich, and went to the door.

"See you tomorrow, Tina," he said.

"Have a good day, Will."

10

Will unlocked the door to his office and entered. The room had a stale smell – perhaps he could get Teri to come in and do a light cleaning. He sat at his desk and ate his sandwich, just staring ahead blankly as he chewed. After eating, he began to doze off. The desk phone rang, startling him. He studied the phone for a moment, debating on whether or not to answer it. After the fourth ring, he leaned forward and picked it up.

"Town of Catherine Police Department."

There was a long pause on the other end followed by a heavy sigh.

"Sheriff Wilson Putner, please."

Will did not recognize the voice.

"Speaking."

"This is Detective John Stone from the State Police Barracks out of Towanda. How are you today?"

"Fine," Will sighed, "what can I do for you, Detective?"

"I was out at County this morning, had to see Buck on a case I'm working on...and you'll never guess what he was working on..."

"I would have no idea."

"...he was working on a frozen male Caucasian that he said came from your town."

Will rolled his eyes as Stone spoke, the detective's sarcasm dripping through every word.

"Didn't think you boys would be interested in a one vehicle MVA..."

"That's funny, Sheriff," Stone snapped, "I thought, no, I assumed that - as a courtesy - a dead body under any circumstances other than natural causes would warrant a call. You did take the time to call Buck..."

"...and I called the County Sheriff's..." Will interrupted.

"...yes, you did call them, "Stone continued, "from what I understand, you downplayed it to them. I take it none of the county boys came up to look at the scene?"

"Nothing to look at but a car and snow."

There was another pause.

"Did you get any pictures at the scene?"

"Nope."

"Why not?"

"Because, it was an accident," Will said, his voice growing terser as he spoke, "there's two, maybe three foot of snow up there. Plus, the wind blowing and drifting."

There is another long pause.

"I'd like to take a look at the scene," Stone finally said.

"You're welcome to it."

"Where's the vehicle?"

Will rubbed his forehead with his free hand.

"Half a block from my office," he said. He could hear Stone's heavy breathing as the Detective was becoming exasperated.

"I want to see that, too."

"You bet."

Stone muttered something that Will couldn't quite understand.

"Excuse me?" Will asked forcefully.

"Condescending fuck, aren't you, Sheriff? I guess your reputation does precede you."

"Well, thank you, Detective. Is there anything else I can do for you?"

Will got no response, only a click from the end of the line.

11

Will left his office and walked up the block past Al's Hardware toward Scooter's Garage. On the scrolling screen across the street at the bank, the temperature blinked 36 degrees.

"Hasn't been this warm in months..." he muttered to himself.

He strolled past the remaining storefronts, casually looking in the windows and occasionally waving to patrons and employees inside. At the end of the street, Scooter's Garage stood before him. Will walked onto the lot and was promptly met by Scooter.

"Mornin', Sheriff," Scooter said from the doorway of his garage.

Will nodded and continued around the garage towards the Toyota. As he arrived at the car, he realized that Scooter had caught up to him.

"How are you, Scooter?"

"Good, Sheriff, good," the mechanic replied, "say, I want you to know I stayed here all night...you know, to watch the car..."

"Well, I appreciate that but you didn't have to..."

"But..."

Will immediately noticed the anxiety on Scooter's face, as the mechanic's eyes started to squint as he looked around. He tried to mouth some words but no sounds came out.

"I do appreciate it, Scooter."

The anxiety on Scooter's face was replaced by relief as he relaxed and smiled. Will opened the driver's side door of the Toyota and knelt down. He

55

noticed a small brown stain on the driver's side window.

"What are you doing," Scooter asked, "looking for evidence? Will brought his hand up and put it next to the stain. The stain itself was an oblong blotch with two small streaks pulled away by gravity and frozen in place by the frigid air.

"Something like that..."

"Did ya find anything?

"Found some blood."

"Really?" Scooter seemed shocked by this revelation. Will turned his attention to the driver's seat and found nothing interesting. He slid up into the seat and stared at the frost covered windshield.

"Yep," Will said quietly in response.

"Anything else?" Scooter was utterly fascinated by this exercise. "It's not every day that we get a dead body in Catherine."

"No, it's not," Will replied. Using a knuckle on his right hand, Will pushed a button on the center console and a small compartment door popped open. The compartment contained papers, a pack of cigarettes, and some coins. Will looked at the mess for a moment then closed the compartment. He then scanned the passenger side of the car; something caught his eye from under the edge of the seat. He took a pen from his pocket and fished the item out from its hiding place. It was a tube sock.

"What is it?" Scooter asked

Will stared at the clean white sock dangling from the end of his pen. It was perfectly straight with a crease centered in the middle of it and had never been worn.

"It's a sock."

"Just one?"

"Yep," Will replied.

"Where's the other one?"

Will leaned over and peeked under the passenger seat. Other than a gum wrapper, it was clean.

"That's a good question...

Will moved out of the car, squatted, and looked under the driver's seat. He dropped the sock and the pen on the driver's seat and, with his left hand, shoved his hand under it. A moment later, his hand emerged, wrapped around something black. Standing, he turned, using both hands to unveil the item.

It was a sheathed knife.

"Now that's a knife," Will said as Scooter leaned in tepidly.

Will unsheathed the eight-inch blade. Scooter stepped a little closer to the car, his eyes focused on the blade.

"Is that, like, a murder weapon or something?" Scooter asked quietly.

"Don't think so," Will answered, "It looks brand new."

Will dropped the knife and the sheath onto the seat next to the pen and sock. He then walked around the car to the passenger side and opened the passenger's door. Bending over, he tapped the button on the glove compartment. The door dropped open and the Sheriff paused before reaching in. He stood, holding up a pistol with two fingers. Scooter stared in wonderment from the other side of the car. Will leaned in, set the gun on the seat, then raised back up.

"Well, it looks like there's more to David Alan Wallace than meets the eye." In his hand, Will held the car registration. Scooter broke out into a huge grin.

12

Will entered his office and closed the door behind him. In his right hand, he held a black garbage bag that Scooter had run back into his garage to get for him. He dropped the partially full bag onto his desk and removed his coat, draping it over his desk chair. He sat in his chair and, grabbing the garbage bag with both hands, dumped the bag onto the desk. The contents - all the items from the car - spill across the desk, with a few pieces of paper that fluttered to the floor.

A cigarette pack tumbled off the desk and landed under Will's chair. He swiped around under the chair, pushing the box with his fingertips before he finally snagged it. He then retrieved the scraps of paper and added them to the pile.

He turned his attention back to the cigarette pack, which felt lumpy and hard as he opened it. Instead of cigarettes, the box contained a small pipe and a tightly wrapped black plastic wad.

"Well now, that changes everything..."

Will held the pipe to his nose and sniffed. Whatever scent had been there was now gone. He set the box and its contents on the corner of the desk, away from the rest of the contents of the bag. His stare held there for a moment and then he moved the knife and the gun over to the same corner.

He began going through the pieces of paper in the pile when his phone began ringing. One piece of paper with handwriting on it held his attention as he let the phone ring. Finally, he answered the phone.

"Town of Catherine Sheriff's Department," he said nonchalantly.

"Will?"

It took a moment before Will recognized the voice.

"Glenda?"

"Hi, Sheriff, sorry to bother you," she said.

"It's no bother," he replied, "what can I do for you?"

"You say that now," Glenda offered as her voice changed to a more serious tone, "it's Amy. I called the number we have for Teri but got no answer. I need you to come and pick Amy up."

Will stopped studying the paper and concentrated on the phone call.

"What happened?"

"There was a fight after phys-ed between Amy and Becky Culver. Both girls have been suspended for three days."

Will's eyes drifted back to the piece of paper.

"I'll be right down to get her."

"Thank you, Sheriff."

Will hung up the phone. He slid the mess together in a tighter pile, pulling the knife, gun and cigarette pack back to the edge of the mess. He opened the top drawer of his desk and put the piece of paper that had fascinated him in the drawer and closed it. The black garbage bag covered the pile in the middle of the desk and Will left his office.

13

Will parked in front of the double doors of the school and entered the foyer, and was greeted by a mural with a roaring tiger. He smiled at it as he ascended the steps to the second floor. The offices were immediately off the stairs to the left with the cafeteria running the entire length of the floor to the right. Large glass windows framed the front of the office along the hallway.

Will noticed Amy sitting in a chair closest to the door. Three seats away, a sullen Becky Culver was sitting with her head down. Past Becky was a long counter and, behind that, two desks with secretaries seated and typing.

Will entered the office, walked to the counter, and immediately went to the Sign In/Sign Out sheet. One of the secretaries looked up and smiled at him. He smiled back and gave her a little wave. Done with the form, he turned and approached Amy.

"Come on, let's go."

Amy looked up at him; her eyes were puffy and red as if she had been crying; her brown hair messed and matted.

"Whatever..."

Amy stood and Will started towards the office door.

"See you in three days, bitch..." Becky mumbled.

"You wanna go outside now, skank?" Amy shouted as she stepped toward Becky.

"Fucking whore!" Becky screamed as she bolted from her seat. Will snagged Amy by her right arm and swung her toward the door. Becky stopped just short of running into the Sheriff.

"Sit down," Will commanded. Holding his grip on Amy with his left hand, he pointed Becky back to her chair with his right. Becky quieted quickly and stepped back to her chair. Will turned to Amy.

"Knock it off."

As if he were leading a perp, he ushered his stepdaughter to the office door and opened it. He released his grip on his her once they were out in the hallway. As they passed the last window before the stairs, Will glanced back at the office. Both secretaries were watching as the Principal, Glenda Donovan, rushed from her office and watched Will take Amy away. He gave Glenda a little wave as they disappeared from her sight.

14

The drive home was painfully slow. Amy sat in the passenger seat of Will's squad car, her head resting against the window. Every so often, Will would glance over at her but her stare remained out the window.

"You wanna tell me what that was about?" Will finally asked. He watched her for a moment as she rolled her eyes. Her face reddened as her eyes began to water. She slowly shook her head. "I asked you a question," Will continued.

"So what," she snapped.

"Jesus Christ, you can't keep acting like this," he shot back.

"What's it matter, anyways," she said as tears streamed down her face.

Will glanced at the road then back at her.

"It does matter," he said with a softer tone.

He turned the car onto Water Street and stopped as Mrs. Mulvaney crossed the street. The lovely old woman smiled and waved at the Sheriff, unaware of the scene she had interrupted. Will forced a smile and waved back. Once moving again, Will looked at Amy.

"It matters, and you do matter. You need to talk to me."

"Why should I talk to you," she said, her voice trembling, "you don't give a fuck about me!"

Will faced the road. He went numb for a moment.

"That's not fair, Amy," he stuttered, "that's not true."

"Isn't it," she replied as she sobbed, "the only reason you're here now is cause they couldn't get ahold of mom!"

Will sucked in a deep breath as he turned onto Felton.

"But I am here now, and I am talking to you."

Through tears, Amy began to laugh.

"Sure, talk to me when I embarrass you in this fucking hell hole of a town!"

Will pulled the car into the driveway and put it in park. He turned and faced her, his hand rested gently on her shoulder.

"You know that I'm always here for you," he said softly.

She sniffled as she stifled her tears.

"Yeah, well, maybe it's too late," she snapped. She opened the car door, stepped out, and slammed the door with attitude. Will watched as she stormed into the house, slamming the front door as well.

"Fuck, that went well…" he muttered sarcastically.

Will sat alone in the car for a few moments, staring at the house. He reached for his door handle when, suddenly, his scanner came to life.

"…10-61 in progress. Suspects are in a blue Chevy Cavalier, license plate number David Zebra 1-9-7-1. Vehicle was last seen heading north on Route 220."

"Shit!"

Will shifted the car into reverse, backed out of the driveway, shifted into gear, and sped away. Will weaved his way through town toward Route 220, which bordered the north end of Catherine. He grabbed his radio and began contact.

"Bradford County Sheriff's Dispatch, this is Catherine Town Sheriff Will Putner. I am en route to assist."

"10-4, Sheriff."

There was a twinge of excitement with Will, both in his voice and his expression. He pulled off Main Street onto County Road 4. A new voice came over the radio.

"No need, Sheriff. Suspects were apprehended in Troy."

Will punched the steering wheel then picked up the radio.

"10-4."

Will dropped the radio, slowed the car, and turned it around, heading back toward Catherine. He drove, ending up on Ketchler Road. Off to the right, the length of the three-mile road, was Ketchler Lake.

The lake, a popular fishing and swimming destination in the area, was empty of customers. Will parked his car alongside the road.

He walked down the embankment to the frozen water's edge. He stood and looked out over the ice, which covered a pretty large swath of the lake. From where he stood, there were a number of ice fishing huts off to his right. Daryl Watson, Kev Walters and old Zeke Muldoon fishing huts were the closest to where Will stood. There were a few other huts further away that he did not recognize.

He took his wallet out of his back pocket, carefully slid a piece of paper from it, and unfolded it. Yellowed and brittle, he held it gingerly.

The paper, a faded newspaper article with the headline BOY STRUCK BY COP, had a grainy picture of the boy to the left of the headline. Will then looked out at the lake with tears welling up in his eyes.

15

Will entered his office just after 1:30 in the afternoon. He had stopped at the diner and grabbed another coffee. He paused before closing the door. Sitting in one of the wooden chairs facing his desk was a large man in a steel-grey uniform. The man did not turn or acknowledge him.

Will shuffled slowly to his desk; he noticed the black garbage bag had been moved slightly.

"If I'd known you were going to be here, I'd have brought you a coffee."

John Stone stood and extended his hand. A large man - not fat, but husky – towered over the sheriff.

"John Stone, State Police."

Will set his coffee down on the desk away from the evidence from the car and weakly grasped Stone's hand. Stone looked at Will's hand, as if he were offended by the handshake.

"I know who you are."

Will sat behind his desk as Stone dropped back down into the stiff wooden chair.

"I was hoping to see what you have on the accident," Stone said as he adjusted in the seat.

Will took a drink of his coffee.

"It's all right here," Will said as he pulled the garbage bag off the pile and dropped it on the floor behind him.

Stone leaned forward a bit.

"What's this?"

"Everything in the car." Will took another drink as Stone looked over the pile carefully as if something were to leap from it.

"Everything?"

"Yep," Will replied.

"You have everything documented?"

"I know what was where," Will answered, slightly annoyed.

"Pictures?" Stone questioned as he took a pen from his pocket and picked through the pile.

"Nope...listen, Detective, I don't see what the big deal is. It's a one car accident. I am working with County on this. All personal effects, next of kin, everything will be handled through them. So, you can chalk this trip up to a lovely drive on a beautiful day."

Will flashed Stone a grin and took another drink of coffee.

"I'd like to see the car and the scene, if that's ok with you, Officer..."

"It's Sheriff."

"I apologize...Sheriff." Stone returned the grin. Will jumped up from his seat.

"Certainly," Will said as he was halfway to the door, "shall we go?"

Stone struggled out of his chair. Will opened the door and held it for the Detective.

"Shall I ride with you, Sheriff?"

Will pushed in the locking knob on the door handle as Stone approached.

"I think we'd better take separate cars," Will answered, "I have an appointment."

"Fine. I'll follow you." Stone brushed past Will and out of the building. Will paused before he followed.

"Well, that makes sense," Will mumbled as he the door behind him.

16

Scooter walked slowly out of his garage, wiping his hands on a greasy rag, after seeing the two police cars park in his lot. His overalls were stained with oil, grease, and dirt, and his face bore some of the marks of his labor as well. He approached Will and Stone as they exited their vehicles.

"Scooter, this is Detective John Stone from the State Police," Will stated as the narrow man neared them. His introduction did little to temper the unease Scooter felt at the sight of Stone. Fumbling to extend his hand to the large Detective, Scooter dropped the greasy rag. Stone dismissed Scooter's hand with a look.

"Mr. Stone...I want...you to know...I haven't left the car...since it got here...you know, watchin' it..."

Stone looked him up and down briefly.

"What's he talking about," Stone asked sternly, "who are you?" Stone turned and glared at Will. "Who is he?"

"He hauled the car out. This is his garage."

Stone faced Scooter again, and the mechanic tried to feign a smile, quite unsuccessfully. His nerves got the better of him and he took a step back.

"The car's over there," Will continued. Stone waited a few moments before he turned and walked towards the Toyota.

"What the hell was that?" Scooter asked once Stone was out of sight.

"Just being a prick," Will replied, his eyes off in the direction of the Toyota, "go back inside. I'll talk to you later."

"What if Captain Tight-ass there wants to talk to me," Scooter wondered, "he looks crazy, Will."

"I'm doing this as a courtesy, Scooter. Nothing more. You won't have to talk to him."

"I thought you said it was an accident..."

"That's what I said..."

"Then what..."

"Go back inside," Will ordered. Scooter glanced past Will to Stone, who was circling the car. Scooter nodded to Will and wandered back to his garage. Will waited a moment then walked over to the car.

"Is this how you found the car?" Stone asked as Will approached.

"Absolutely. Why?"

"None of this damage occurred while you were removing the car from the scene?"

Will's face reddened with anger.

"It is as it was," Will answered in a terse voice.

"There's heavy damage to the front of the vehicle and substantial damage to the undercarriage." Stone continued to circle the car then stopped and gestured at the passenger side. "But the damage here is not consistent with the other damage. It is behind the passenger's door. Not on the door, or in front of the door, but behind it."

"Maybe that is pre-existing damage."

"Maybe...but the oxidation is about the same as the other damage."

Stone opened the passenger door with a gloved hand and dropped down on the seat, his feet on the ground outside the car. He flipped down both visors, opened the glove box, and checked the ashtray. Finding nothing, he stood and closed the door.

"I'd like to see the scene now," Stone demanded.

17

Teri opened the door to the Sheriff's office, removed her key from it, and stepped in quickly. She shivered as she tried to brace herself from the cold she had just escaped, and folded her arms across her chest.

"Of course, you're not here," she said to herself, "why can't you be napping in your chair?"

She walked over to Will's desk and looked at the plastic garbage bag covering it. She opened the top drawer and grabbed a pen and paper. She started to write when her cell phone went off. She glanced at the caller ID.

"Shit, Billie, I'm on my way back to work..."

Without answering the phone, she tucked her cell phone and the piece of paper into a coat pocket, dropped the pen in the desk drawer, and ran out of the office.

18

Will pulled his car to the side of the road, his passenger side tires on the packed-snow shoulder. He squinted, what with the sun shining brightly on this cloudless winter day directly in front of him. He glanced at the outside thermometer hanging above his rearview mirror: 36 degrees.

Suddenly, Stone's car pulled up behind his. Will watched as Stone quickly got out of his vehicle and zipped up his coat. Will sighed and stepped from his car, and looked out over the large field before him. With the bright sun and slowly melting snow, it appeared as if everything had a sheet of ice blanketing it. Stone approached Will, his eyes beginning to water from the cold.

"So, this is it?"

"Yep," Will replied as he reached into his coat pocket and pulled out his winter gloves. In front of his car, large hardened clumps of snow lay scattered about. The trench that Will, Daryl, and Scooter left when they hauled the car out was before them.

"I take it," Stone said, his voice breaking as a brief gust of wind kicked up, "it was down there?"

"You are the Detective."

Stone glared at Will for a moment, turned, and walked back towards his car. He spent a few minutes studying the road, the field, and various angles. He then walked past Will and stepped down the embankment into the field. Will shrugged as he watched Stone traipse through the deep snow before he followed him in.

"Watch your step," Will offered, "the snow's still pretty deep."

"I'm fine, Sheriff," Stone snapped from ahead of Will. After six full steps, Stone sunk into the soft snow up to his thigh. He tipped sideways, awkwardly. Will moved past Stone on the Detective's left.

"Shit," Stone huffed as Will strode away from him. Will stopped and looked back at him.

"Lean back a little then pull your leg out."

"I know what I'm doing," Stone said as he struggled.

"I can see that." Will continued down the hill until he reached the pines. He turned and watched Stone continue to struggle, sinking both legs up to his thighs some thirty feet past the first incident.

Finally, Stone reached the pines. He was panting heavily, and a glaze of frozen sweat frosted his forehead. Will turned away from Stone to the pines and smiled.

"Well, as you can see, this is where the car was found."

Attempting to catch his breath, Stone glared at Will, his face red with anger. Stone then looked back toward the road.

"How the hell did you see it from up there?" he asked as he bent over and started brushing snow from his pants.

"I didn't. A local farmer spotted it."

"Really," Stone said as he straightened back up, "I'd like to talk to him."

"I don't think so..."

Stone pivoted and stepped directly in front of Will.

"I'm asking for a little cooperation, Sheriff."

"This isn't your case, Detective," Will stated calmly as the larger man hovered over him, "this is my case, which is why I'm handling it through County. You want courtesy, I am being courteous. But this is as far as it goes. You have nothing to do here. Nothing."

A low rumble started as Will spoke and grew progressively louder after Will stopped talking. Both men turn towards the road. A tractor appeared in view behind their cars.

Daryl was standing on his tractor, waving emphatically.

"Who's that?"

"That would be the farmer," Will answered. Without hesitation, Will started his walk to the road. Stone exhaled a loud sigh.

"Look around all you want down here," Will continued without looking back, "when you are done, you can go."

Stone watched Will walk up the burrowed-out trench towards the road before he started inspecting the area where the car was found. Will walked confidently up the hill without looking back to see if Stone was following. As Will approached the road, Daryl stepped down off his tractor.

"Howdy, Will," Daryl exclaimed enthusiastically. Will looked past Daryl at the tractor.

"Daryl. Again with the tractor?

"Moved Mabel's snow today. By the time we was done yesterday, it was late. Supper time."

"That it was."

"Say, is that the fella from the State Police," Daryl asked as he looked over Will's shoulder. Will turned and looked in the direction that caught Daryl's eye. Stone was struggling through the deep snow as he ascended the hill.

"You're more perceptive than he is," Will said quietly. Daryl turned red and chuckled.

"Scooter called me and told me there was a big fella lookin' around. What's he lookin' for?

Will paused and drew in a deep breath.

"Trouble."

Neither man spoke for a few moments as Stone sunk in another snow pit. Finally, Daryl shook his head.

"It was an accident, Will, right?"

Will paused as they watched Stone free himself.

"You head on home, Daryl. You don't need to talk to anyone but me. Tomorrow, if you get a shot, come on down and give a statement. I'll file a report, pass it on to County, and that'll be it."

Daryl nodded, boarded his tractor, and left the scene just as Stone reached the road.

"Is there anything else before you head back, Detective?"

Stone marched to within inches of Will's face, fury in his eyes. The veins in his forehead are throbbing. It is all he can do not to take a swing at the Sheriff.

"Play this fucking game out, Sheriff, but know one thing...I know who you are. I know what happened. Do you really want to dredge all that up and make this bigger than it is?"

Will stared intently at Stone, not wavering one bit.

"Get the fuck out of my town."

19

Will opened the door to his office, coffee in hand. He casually flipped his keys onto his desk as he walked past, heading for the small storage closet in the back of the room. After a moment of rummaging through, he produced a cardboard box and walked back to his desk.

Bright sunlight broke through a sliver of the window shade, catching him right in the eyes as he sat down. He rolled his chair to the side a little, and put his coffee cup on the desk.

Sliding the garbage bag off the pile onto the floor, Will looked over the items one last time. He started collecting all the papers and putting them in the bottom, then the sock, followed by the gun and the knife. When he came to the cigarette pack, he held it in his hand for a few moments and looked it over.

Satisfied, he placed the bulging cigarette pack into the box.

"Marker...marker..." Will opened the top drawer of his desk, grabbed a marker out of instinct, and paused.

The piece of paper he had placed in there earlier was gone.

He scribbled "WALLACE" on the side of the box, pushed the drawer shut, and whipped the marker across the room in anger.

"Fuck!"

He covered the box, carried it to the back storage room, and then stormed out of the office.

20

Will gripped the steering wheel so tightly that his knuckles turn white as he drove. Still seething about the paper, and about John Stone, angered him like he hadn't been for so many years. This was his case, his shot to be relevant again.

His mind wandered as that horrible day from his past returned. The call had come in for an officer assist, there had been a three-car accident involving a deputy. The dispatcher had called for multiple buses to transport the injured. Will was on Saco Road, just off 220, when the call came in. His light bar lit up, siren blaring, Will sped in the direction of the call.

And the boy darted out of the road from between two cars...

Will's car ran over something in the road, creating a loud THUNK, which snapped him back into the moment. He stopped quickly and shifted the rearview mirror, only to see part of a tree branch crumpled in the road behind him. With the brake released, he drove around Catherine for nearly an hour, then departed town for the countryside. He turned onto Fuller Road and parked the car. He instinctively reached for his coffee cup but it was not there.

"Shit," he muttered.

He rubbed his forehead, punched the steering wheel, then leaned his head back and closed his eyes.

21

Will drove home slowly, as night had crept in while he dozed alongside the road, and a light snow began to fall.

He entered his house through the kitchen door. Inside, it was dark save for the light that was on over the kitchen sink. He went to the refrigerator and grabbed a beer and, after looking for a moment, a few slices of American cheese. Grabbing a loaf of bread from the breadbox, Will plucked two slices from the bag, and returned the loaf to the box.

As he took the first bite from his cheese sandwich, the living room light came on. He opened the beer and took a swig.

Teri enters the kitchen from the living room.

"Where have you been?"

"Working." Will took another bite of the sandwich as he leaned against the counter. Teri emitted a disgusted, disbelieving sigh.

"Working? Really, you sticking with that?" Teri moved to the sink and tightened her robe over her shorts and tee-shirt. She then began taking care of the clean dishes in the strainer.

"I'm not sticking with anything. I was working."

"Somebody's cat missing," she snapped as she turned to face him, "some kids running around the cemetery? What's so god damned important that you can't be home with your family at night? Or did you forget you have a family?"

Will swallowed a drink of beer.

"Ah, Teri, that's not fair..."

Teri slammed a frying pan on the counter, loud enough to wake the neighborhood.

"That's always your out, isn't it? 'It's not fair...that's not fair.' No, Will, it's not fair! It's not fair to me and Amy! By the way, bang up job you did with her today. Did you even try..."

"She wouldn't talk to me..."

"Did you actually try to talk to her," Teri spoke, her voice rising, "or were you your always condescending ass and talk down to her?"

"I wanted to hear her out but she didn't want to talk to me."

"Right. And I wonder why that is, Will? Can you tell me because, like her, I need to be enlightened by your wisdom..."

Will tossed the rest of his sandwich in the garbage can next to the door and swallowed the remainder of his beer.

"Oh, I can't wait to hear this," Teri continued as she crossed her arms.

Will dropped the bottle into the trash, looked Teri in the eye for a moment, then opened the back door.

"Oh, what, are you leaving? Running away?"

"Going to the shop," Will said without facing her.

"Well, isn't that like you. Run away." She paused as he stopped in the doorway. That brief moment lit a fire under her. "When was the last time you talked to me, huh? You know, more than two words in passing?"

Will started to take a step then stopped, his back still to Teri. Sensing his weakness, she pounced.

"When was the last time you touched me, Will? Huh? When was the last time you fucked me? Do you remember that?"

Will stepped outside and slammed the door behind him. He was three steps toward the shop when the kitchen door swung open behind him.

"Nothing to say? You're not getting off that easy!"

Will turned and faced his wife, his voice a low growl.

"You don't talk...you bitch. Tape yourself and listen to it - you're not that interesting. Oh, and as for Amy, I've tried. But who gives a shit, she's not my daughter, she's yours."

Teri froze in the doorway, stunned, mouth agape. All the color had drained from her face as tears began to flow from her eyes. She stepped back into the kitchen and slammed the door. Seconds later, the living room light went off. Will looked at the ground then back at the house.

"Dipshit, dumbshit," Will muttered to himself. He turned and made his way to his shop, the light fluffy snowflakes patting his face as he went. He unlocked the shop door, reached in and hit the light switch, illuminating the whole workspace.

As he shut the door, he glanced back at the house. From her second story bedroom window, Amy was watching him.

Crying.

22

Will did not work on his big project, the cabinet; instead, he is sat on a stool next to his work bench. A notepad and pen in his hands, he took a brief moment to ponder, then wrote onto the pad. Every once in a while, he would glance up from his writing and look at the cabinet with his gun, shells, and duffel bag.

23

Amy sat in her bed, her fingers rolling over the fur of a toy stuffed rabbit she had since she was six years old. The rabbit had been one of the first gifts Will had given her. She crossed her legs above the blankets, stared at the rabbit, and began to cry.

There was a light rap at her door.

"Amy, honey, may I come in," her mother asked softly. Amy glanced at the door then back at her stuffed companion. "Amy, sweetie, I know you're up..."

The door opened ever so slightly and Teri peered in.

"I'm really not in the mood to talk," Amy said through tears as Teri shut the door behind her and walked to the bed. As she sat next to her daughter on the edge of the bed, she reached over and brushed hair away from Amy's eyes.

"Oh, baby, you heard that…"

Amy sniffled and Teri slid in and wrapped an arm around her, pulling her tight. "Oh, sweetie, you know he didn't mean it."

"I heard what he said..."

"He didn't mean it," Teri said as she tried to comfort her daughter.

"Why would he say that?" Amy sniffled again after she spoke. Teri frowned before answering.

"He's mad at me, sweetie, not you."

"Do you hate each other?"

Teri was quick to respond.

"No, baby, we don't hate each other. We're just…under a lot of stress right now."

Amy flopped down onto the bed, her head on the pillow as she now picked at the rabbit's faux fur.

"But I heard you down there…you're right, he doesn't talk to us anymore. It's like he hates us."

"He doesn't hate us," Teri interjected, "he's busy." She quickly smiled as she tried to deflect the conversation. "Do remember going to the State Fair, the two of you riding all the rides…"

"That was two years ago," Amy interrupted, "and over the past few months, he doesn't even come home at night. And when he does, he spends all of his time in his stupid shop."

Teri started to tear up and looked away for a moment. She gained control of herself and pasted on a smile.

"He loves you."

There was a pause before Amy replied.

"But, does he love you?"

Teri, not knowing how to answer her daughter's question, forced a weak smile as she, too, started to cry.

24

Will entered his house through the kitchen door just after two in the morning. He slipped into his bedroom and stood at the foot of the bed, watching Teri as she slept on her side facing the window. Ted was stretched out in Will's spot, his head on Will's pillow. After a moment, Will walked around the bed, softly touched Teri's face, and gently kissed her forehead. He then placed a piece of paper on the nightstand next to her head, leaning it against the alarm clock. Will then walked to Amy's room, placed a similar piece of paper on her pillow, and left the room.

25

Will was stretched out in his desk chair, reclined, with his feet up on his desk. He had arrived at the station just before three in the morning and was asleep in his chair minutes later.

He was dozing, a groggy half-sleep that kept him somewhat restless. After many hours of adjusting in his chair, suddenly, the door to his office opened. Will struggled to opens his eyes.

A figure dressed in brown approached him slowly.

"Will."

"David."

County Sheriff David Havens stood opposite Will for a moment before sitting in one of the uncomfortable wooden chairs around the desk. He removed his hat and ran his fingers through his short, salt and pepper hair. Will tried sitting up, and cranked his head both ways, cracking his sore neck.

"You look like shit," Havens said firmly.

"Ah, so much for the pleasantries," Will said as he dropped his feet heavily to the floor, "it's nice to see you, too." He sat forward in his chair, leaning on his desk.

"Sleeping in the office now...overworking a case or trouble at home?"

"Both."

Will sat back in his chair as Havens emitted a noise that sounded like a hum.

"We need to talk."

"Okay?"

Uncomfortable, Havens adjusted himself in his chair before speaking.

"I received a call yesterday. Want to guess from whom?"

"None of my business any of the women you have calling..."

"Not even close," Havens interrupted, "John Stone, State Police. Says he wants to have a chat with me. Care to venture a guess what it was about?"

"Is he the one selling tickets to the Policeman's golf tournament?"

"That may be you before this is over," Havens continued, "nah, he's jabbering away about some MVA in your little hamlet here and claims that I'm working with you to shut him out of the investigation. That starting to make any sense to you?"

Will stretched and looked around, as if he were bored by this conversation.

"I need coffee..."

"Care to explain?"

"It's a drink, caffeine, you have in the..."

"About the call," Havens spoke, his tone still terse. His face remained calm with its façade but was beginning to redden.

"Nah, that's pretty much it."

"Did you tell Buck not to talk to the State Police?"

"I may have suggested," Will stammered. Havens adjusted himself in his chair as his tone became more serious.

"Jesus Christ, Will, what the fuck is going on here? Why are you rubbing the Staties the wrong way on a one car crash?"

"I did my job, David!" There was an awkward pause as Will composed himself. "I called it in. I called your office. And by the time I leave today, you will have my report. You want the car, you can have it. The kid's box of shit, it's yours. But this...this is mine. Mine."

Will's eyes locked with the County Sheriff's as the latter stiffened in his chair.

"You're not cracking, are you," Havens asked, "I mean, all these years in this little shit town, it hasn't fucked you all up, has it?"

Will looked away.

"I'm fine."

"You know, you have no one else to blame but yourself," Havens continued, "you...put yourself here."

Will's face reddened, anger sweeping through him.

"I'm not talking about what happened twenty years ago."

"I am," Havens said, leaning forward, "it seems like every few years we have to have this conversation. It was an accident. You were cleared."

"And Pierson, and the State Police, wouldn't drop it..."

"But they did drop it, Will. Over and done with. It was your choice not to come back to County."

Will's eyes began to moisten as he stifles a tear.

"The boy..."

"I know, Will, the boy died," Havens said, his voice not as harsh, "it was an accident. I know."

The room grew eerily silent. Will glanced all around the room without making any eye contact with Havens, who focused completely on the man opposite him.

"I'm fine here."

"Sure," Havens said snidely, "you look it." He paused, then glared through Will. "How's the family?"

Will lowered his head, shook it slowly, and chuckled.

"How long have we known each other?" Havens continued.

"Long time..."

"Since high school. And I've always looked out for you. Always. So, what I'm about to say is painful for me to say." Havens paused and exhaled a breath

116

audibly. "You're a loser, Will. You've got nothing. No ambition, no career, nothing worth a shit."

"Now wait," Will spoke, shocked.

"No, let me finish," Havens demanded, "your wife, Teri, is a loser. Worthless. Tell me, what is she good for, really? Nothing. She didn't finish high school, can't hold a steady job for longer than six months. Where is she at now...that restaurant over in Canton? And that kid of hers, Amy? Nothing but trouble."

Will looked away, then back at his old friend. He was trying to compose himself but his hand was shaking slightly and his eyes were beginning to water.

"David..."

"And, so, what have you got? This? You know, every two years a vote comes up on whether to dissolve this office and let County handle it. I can only keep this up for so long, Will. How long before all this goes away? How long?"

"May I speak now?"

"Have at it."

"This isn't exactly how I envisioned it but you know what, David? It's my life," Will seethed, a quiet rage within his voice, "this is my office in my town. And until they shut me down, it's mine. You have a lot of balls coming into my office and talking to me like that."

"It's something you need to hear."

Will ignored Haven's comment as if he didn't hear it.

"And, as for my family, I'm letting that slide once. Once." Will paused briefly and locked eyes with Havens, "consider that a favor to an old friend. There will be no mention of my family ever again."

Havens noticed the tears welling up in Will's eyes.

"Fair enough." Havens stood and grabbed his hat from the seat next to him. "One more thing...if you ever want to invoke the County Sheriff's office into anything in the future, call me first. I don't like surprises."

"Fine."

Havens paused and watched Will for a moment before he walked to the door.

"Goodbye, David."

Havens turned and looked at Will for the last time.

"Goodbye, Will."

26

Will drove through Catherine and ended up on County Road 7, a road on the outskirts of town. He parked the car on the shoulder, stepped out, and sucked in a deep breath of cool, morning air. The trees were rustling off in the distance; the sky was filling with dark grey clouds. Will looked up and down the road.

"What were you doing out here, Wallace," Will muttered to himself, "why Catherine...and why has no one reported you missing?"

After a few moments of studying the area, Will walked back to his car and drove up to the crossroad where Daryl's farm sat, and turned left. He drove half a mile and made another left onto Fuller Road. He slowed to a crawl then stopped, parking his car on the shoulder, part-way down the road. This short, connecting road contained two mobile homes and one farm house. The farm, the trailers, and the land on this road were owned by the Fuller family. They resided in the farm house; the trailers were rentals.

At that moment, Will was parked a little more than 100 yards away from the first residence, a blue and white mobile home that had a brown Dodge minivan parked in the driveway and some children's toys scattered about the yard. Will sat and watched the trailer for more than an hour before heading back to the office.

27

Will sat at his desk, his work phone in hand.

"Yeah, Buck, it's Will returning your call."

"Hey, trouble," Buck said with a bit of joy in his voice.

"Funny..."

"I thought so," the coroner said as he chuckled, "hey, your kid there - Wallace - died from massive internal injuries. Under usual circumstances, I'd say he suffered a lot."

"What do you mean by that?"

"Well, that kid was higher than the moon."

"With what," Will asked as he grabbed a pen and scrap of paper and began writing.

"Short answer, meth," Buck answered, "also had traces of marijuana, hydrocodone, and Percocet. I'm guessing when he went off that road and hit the tree, he smacked his head real good. He had a fracture near the left temporal lobe. Thing is, he was so high, I don't think he realized he was bleeding to death."

"How long could he have been alive?"

"Probably hours...shock setting in combined with the cold and all the drugs...hell, a long time."

Will scribbled furiously on the paper then paused and looked up, staring blankly.

"Any evidence of other physical trauma…a fight or anything like that?"

There was a brief pause before Buck answered. "No. Why?"

"Just wondering…"

Will jotted one more line down.

123

"Well, I appreciate it, Buck," Will continued.

"Again, this is just the cursory exam." Buck said, "we'll have a more in-depth procedure by the end of the week. There's just so much to this DB."

"Thanks for the heads up, really. This helps."

"You act like it wasn't some junkie that ran off the road..."

"Nah, that's probably all it was," Will surmised, "I'm just curious as to why he was in Catherine."

"Probably a couple of wrong turns off the highway. Hell, Will, you know how turned around you can get once you get up in the hills?"

"Yeah, I know that. Just odd that Wallace doesn't having a Missing Persons out on him." Will sighed and dropped the pen onto the desk. "Give me a call when you hear anything else."

"Will do," Buck replied, "take care."

"You, too."

Will dropped the receiver down in the cradle. He stared at the phone for a moment, his elbows on the desk and his hands balled into fists in front of his mouth. After a moment, he tapped a button on the phone. A recorded voice spoke after a beep.

"You have two messages. The first message at 12:53 p.m, 'Hey Will, this is Buck, give...'" Will tapped a button on the phone. "Message erased. The next message at 1:14 p.m. 'Hi...Will, I tried your cell but you left it home today...so, you're going to have a bunch of missed calls from me on there...I found your note...and I talked to Amy. We need this, Will. We need to be a family again. Dinner tonight. I took half a day and Amy doesn't have anything after school so...'" There is a long pause, then "'we'll see you for dinner. I...love you.'"

There was a click as Teri hung up.

Will stared at the phone, a tear welling up in one eye.

28

Will rolled his car to a stop in front of the Daisy Mini Mart as a light snow began to fall. He entered the store and nodded to the cashier.

"Hey, Sheriff."

"Jody," Will replied as he crossed through the store. She stopped counting cigarette packs on the rack next to the counter and smiled broadly. A buzzer went off and the clerk left her post behind the register and walked over to the deli area, where she opened a pizza oven and slid a pie from it into a box. Will continued to the cooler and grabbed a six pack of Pepsi. He made his way to the register with purpose, setting the soda on the counter as Jody brought the pizza to him.

"Will that be all," the cashier asked. From the corner of his eye, Will spied a small rack with flowers.

"Not quite…"

29

Darkness had descended on Catherine as Will pulled into his driveway. He sat for a moment, staring at his house. All of the windows glowed from lights and lamps, and he watched as Teri and Amy moved from the living room into the dining room.

He left the car with his bounty in hand, and crossed to the back of the house, entering through the kitchen door. Teri and Amy both greeted him as he entered - Teri with a hug and a kiss, Amy with a smile. He set the pizza and soda on the kitchen counter, then dug into the Daisy Mini Mart plastic bag and retrieved two roses. He handed one to Teri, then crossed the room and handed the other to Amy.

"For the women in my life," he said softly, almost shyly. Amy had tears well up in her eyes as

Teri rushed over and threw her arms around him with a tight hug.

"I love you," she whispered in his ear. Will wrapped his muscular arms around her and pulled her close.

"I love you, too," he said. They released after a long moment, and both looked at Amy, who was wiping tears from her face.

"I…uh…am pretty hungry," she said, changing the tone, "can we eat?"

Will and Teri laughed, and Amy grabbed plates while Amy carried the pizza into the dining room. Will watched the two work in unison for a moment before taking off his coat and boots, and joining them. As he entered the dining room, Amy was already seated and serving up slices. Teri approached Will and embraced him again.

"What you wrote was the sweetest thing I've ever read," she whispered as she leaned in.

"I meant every word," Will replied, loud enough for Amy to hear. Teri kissed his cheek, smiled, and sat down.

All three were quiet as they started eating. Finally, Amy broke the silence.

"So, anything exciting happening?"

Will and Teri looked at her, with Amy's eyes focused on her step-father. He was in mid-chew, and so he hurried until he swallowed.

"Uh, actually, there was a car found up on County Road Seven...well, off County Road Seven. Way off."

"Abandoned?" Teri asked.

"Not quite," Will continued, "it had been there awhile...for months. Driver was dead."

"Oh God," Teri gasped.

"How come no one saw it?"

Will turned and looked at Amy, who was suddenly engrossed in this story.

"That's a good question. You may be a good cop yet." He paused before answering. "It was hidden in a patch of pines and buried under snow."

"Oh God," Teri repeated. Will glanced her way and smiled.

"I think you said that already."

"Snow? How long had it been there," Amy inquired.

"Months."

"Male or female driver?" Amy asked. Will laced his fingers and rested his elbows on the table, intent on satisfying her queries.

"Young male."

"Oh, his poor family," Teri said, her tone now worried.

"He was a drug runner," Will added, "at least, I think he was a drug runner."

"Really," Teri wondered, "here, in Catherine?"

"It's not about highly dense area of population, Teri. It's about the ease of distribution. These criminals like to set up in out of the way places, where they will attract little to no attention. As for this area, we are close to the New York border, Route 86 will take them to New York City, 15 south towards Scranton, 14 north to the thruway and they can hit Syracuse, Rochester, Buffalo…"

"So, Catherine is a hub," Amy interrupted. A big smile crept across Will's face.

"It appears that, yes, Catherine is a hub. At least, for now."

Teri had a worried look cross her face. She looked at her daughter.

"You don't know anyone who sells drugs or uses drugs, do you?

"Mom!"

"I never really thought something like this could happen in Catherine," she spoke, not reacting to Amy.

"Remember that report we watched on Dateline years ago," Will responded, "the one on identity theft? Do you remember where that was?"

Teri stared at her husband blankly.

"Penn Yan, New York," Will continued after a moment, "a little town about an hour north of us. And all of that black market shit was flowing through there. Honestly, most small towns aren't equipped to handle something so large, and most would never even look for it."

"So, what are you going to do about it," Amy asked. Will looked at her, the smile evaporating from his face.

"I have to go...shortly. I think I know where it's coming from."

"Will..."

Will turned to his wife.

"This is mine, Teri. I know...what you are going to say but this...this is mine. After tonight, I will be here. Every night, and that's a promise. Hell, tomorrow, we've got that big game up in Athens, right?"

Will looked at Amy, who broke out in a big grin while taking a bite of pizza.

"I need to do this for me...for us, and for the town."

Amy dropped the slice onto her plate, stood and walked around the table, and wrapped her arms around Will's shoulders.

"Go get 'em," she said as she planted a kiss on his cheek.

30

Will rummaged through the open cabinet in his shop. The light above him flickered, and he paused, looking up at it until it stopped strobing and straightened out. With his attention back on task, he grabbed the shotgun, shells, binoculars and the black duffel from his cabinet. He walked them out and placed them on the front passenger seat of his car, which he had pulled down by the shop.

After he glanced at the house - with the only light coming from the living room at the front of it – he placed the shotgun in a clip attached to the dash. He then slung the duffel over the passenger seat into the back seat, and rested the binoculars on the dashboard.

He wandered back to the shop, hit the light switch, encasing it in darkness. As he walked back to the car, he took one long look at the house. Teri stood in the back doorway, a cup of coffee cradled in both hands. Will smiled her way. She leaned to her right, resting against the doorframe, then smiled and gave him a friendly wave.

Will placed his Sheriff's hat on his head, wrapped his hand around the brim, and gave her a serious look. She giggled. Will broke out in a smile, winked at her, climbed into the car, and backed out of the driveway.

31

The darkness seemed especially black, with only a quarter moon in the sky surrounded by brilliant stars. Will navigated through town to its outskirts, and finally turned onto Fuller Road.

Will parked where he had before – down the road from the first trailer. Through his binoculars, he scanned the mobile home and its exterior. Along with the Dodge minivan that had been there before, there were now three more cars in the driveway - a green Honda, a black Toyota, and a blue Ford pickup truck. Most of the lights were on inside the house. Will sat in the car for twenty minutes, watching the trailer from a distance.

"Stone...Stone...Stone," Will muttered to himself, "why haven't you hit this place yet?"

As he watched through the various windows, Will counted four men, one woman, and one baby. After observing the trailer for a while, Will noticed the woman carry the baby down the hall. A light went on at the end of the trailer, stayed on for a few minutes, then went out.

A twinge of excitement raced through Will as a smile crossed his face, the binoculars dropping on the passenger seat beside him. He glanced into the back seat, then put his hand on the shotgun.

With his lights off, he inched the car up the road past the trailer. He parked on the shoulder of the road, partially blocked from view by a small hedgerow and out of sight of the trailer. He flicked the switch turning off the dome light before he stepped out of the car. The trunk popped open and Will grabbed his bulletproof vest on and slipped it over his head, securing the

Velcro side straps. He checked his pistol - full clip - and quickly loaded five shells into the shotgun.

"Time to put yourself back on the map, old boy," Will mumbled, attempting to psych himself up. Will clipped his badge to his belt as he looked at the trailer through the scrawny limbs, then crossed the road. He walked quickly until he reached the driveway.

He squatted and moved from behind the truck to the Honda until he was finally behind the Dodge minivan. Crouched no more than forty feet from the kitchen window, Will peeked around the van.

Three of the men sat around the kitchen table. The fourth entered the kitchen, set something on the table, and walked out of the room.

Will hurried around the van and hustled along the front of the trailer until he was by the door. The stench coming from the trailer - which smelled like sulfur mixed with rotting meat - was almost unbearable, causing Will to wince and nearly gag. He gathered himself and shook his head ever so slightly as closed his eyes tightly.

"How the fuck am I getting in there?"

After a long pause, Will turned and faced the front of the trailer. He sucked in a deep breath, exhaled, and rapped ever so lightly on the door.

Nothing.

He waited, then rapped again with the knuckles on his left hand. From his vantage point, he saw the shadows of the inhabitants from the large kitchen and living room windows moving about out in the snow around him. He could hear voices as they moved.

Footsteps grew louder as someone walked closer to the door.

"It's nothing...probably just the wind," a male voice said just before the door opened a crack.

Will pivoted into the doorway quickly, his shotgun pointed squarely at the chest of young, scruffy man wearing a Metallica tee-shirt and shorts.

"Police! Move back! Hands where I can see them!"

The shocked man backed up as Will climbed the three steps into the trailer. He stood in the living room and quickly took in his surroundings. The living room stretched to his left, with bland, worn tan shag carpeting under horrifying dark blue drapes, and green painted paneling on the walls. The woman he had watched carrying the baby was sitting on a wooden-armed couch behind a filthy glass coffee table, a pile of money scattered about it.

Off to Will's right, two men stood next to the kitchen table. One was a short man bald man wearing only blue jeans and the other was a pale, skinny man in grimy clothes. Slowly, they tried inching together to hide the stash on the table.

"Dude, relax," Metallica said slowly.

"Shut up!" Will shouted. Will's eyes scanned the rooms again. "Where's the other guy?"

The shirtless man in the kitchen started fidgeting. "What, man, we're the only ones here..."

Will swung the shotgun toward the two men in the kitchen.

"No, no, no!" the man screamed.

"That how you want to play this out," Will stated calmly as the two men began to shake, "okay, out here...now!"

The two walked carefully from the kitchen, their arms raised slightly, until they were standing next to the man in the Metallica shirt.

"You can't just come barging into my house," the skinny woman with a small pot belly yelled from the couch, "you need a warrant."

"I don't need shit," Will snapped. As he spoke, a flash caught his eye from the dark hallway to his far left, an exit from the living room that led to the bedrooms. Following the flash there was a pop. Will went to swing his shotgun but the impact of the bullet hitting him in the side knocked him off his feet. His finger instinctively squeezed the trigger.

The pale skinny man from the kitchen suddenly disappears from Will's sight, a red spray on the wall behind where he had been standing.

The woman screamed.

Will hit the floor and rolled onto his side. Aching with each breath, Will turned towards the hall. A tall, rugged bearded man wearing a t-shirt and shorts, emerged from the hallway, a 12-gauge shotgun in his

145

hands. He fired again, and the buckshot sprayed into the kitchen behind Will.

Will slides the pump on his shotgun and fires.

The top of the bearded man's head exploded in a volcano of scalp, hair, brains and blood on the wall and ceiling behind him. The body stood for a moment as the gun dropped slowly to the floor before it dropped to its knees then falls forward, sans head.

The woman screamed uncontrollably as she lunged from the couch towards her husband. She touched his chest, glanced back at Will and scrambled for the dead man's gun.

Will fired his shotgun.

The blast hit the woman in her torso, between the ribs and stomach. Her screams became horrid shrieks. Will propped himself up on one elbow as he watched the woman thrashed against the far wall, just beyond the couch. Her yellow shirt quickly became red. A piece of skin flapped in unison with the sounds of her death.

Metallica and the shirtless man scrambled to the coffee table, sweeping money into plastic grocery bags.

"Hands," Will commanded as he attempted to stand. Both men stopped, dropping what they had as they thrust their hands high into the air. Will staggered and dropped back to one knee and toppled over.

Both men bolted for the door, each grabbing a plastic bag of money on the way. Metallica reached the door first and leapt out the door. The shirtless man got to the doorway as Will fired his last round. The second man disappeared out the door.

Using the shotgun, Will pulled himself to his feet. He staggered to the door, unholstering his sidearm as he went.

The shirtless man sprawled out, face down in the snow and grass in front of the door, a pool of blood forming around him. A bag of money laid open a few feet away from his body and a few bills fluttered across the lawn.

The green Honda started up. Will dropped his shotgun, raised his handgun and fired. The rear driver's side window shatters.

The Honda, blocked in by the Toyota, sped backwards and slammed into the car, swerved forward and looped through the yard, bottoming out as it hit the road.

Will grabbed the bag of money and tried to run to his car, limping as he went. As he opened his car door, the sound of a baby crying echoed from the trailer.

32

Will ran his car wide open, with only his headlights on – no red and whites flashing. The Honda fishtailed in the slushy snow and Will eased off the gas and relaxed his grip on the steering wheel, carefully guiding his car around the curve. Even though he was nearly an eighth of a mile behind, the Sheriff was slowly gaining.

The Honda had turned off Fuller Road and Will had approached the "T" intersection with the expertise of a racecar driver. Now heading into the hills of Bradford County, Will's prey swerved from time to time, allowing the lawman to pick up ground.

The Honda suddenly jerked to the left as it approached Baker Road, corrected, and shot off down it with Will in pursuit. The lead car blew past the first intersection - County Road Five - and nearly lost control. The driver of the Honda barely slowed as the car went sideways. A quick flick of the wheel as the car hit a sanded patch of road and the Honda was off again at full speed. Will's hand remained steady on the wheel. He had closed to within a hundred yards of the Honda.

"Where ya going, bub," Will said, a smile crossing his face. He seemed to be enjoying the chase.

The Honda slowed a bit, slid, and sped up the next crossroad, which was County Road Seven.

"What are the odds," Will said as he cut the corner sharply. Seconds later, the Honda followed by the Sheriff's car blew past Daryl Watson's farm. Up the hill they continued past the patch of pines and, finally, past Mabel Conner's farm at the end of the road. The Honda banked right on Veranza Road and Will followed, now within a dozen car lengths.

"Short road, asshole," Will muttered, "which way are you going to go...to town or to the lake?"

The Honda's brake lights came on quickly and, at the last possible second, turned left onto McKraken Road. Will slid his car around the intersection and mashed his foot down on the gas pedal. He had closed to within five car lengths. A clearing in the night sky opened the half-moon up over Ketchler Lake, which was on Will's right side. From the corner of his eye, the dark blotches of the fishing huts caught his eye.

He reached for the car radio.

"County...this is..."

The Honda's brake lights come on suddenly, and the car slides sideways. Will dropped the radio as the taillights of the Honda became bigger and brighter. Will then saw the herd of deer in the road.

The Honda slammed into a doe and slid off the right side of the road, coming to a halt against a small bank of snow. Will cranked his wheel sharply to the right, just missing three other doe. His driver's side fender scraped the bumper of the Honda, continued down the hill at full speed, gained air along a ridge, and smashed through the ice into the frigid Ketchler Lake.

33

It took less than a minute for the car to be submerged. Moments later, the lights on the Sheriff's car went out.

34

The air was crisp the next morning. The sun was in full display with hardly a cloud in the sky. However cold it was, it did not deter people from the lake.

Kev Walters, whose long grey beard swung down over his large down coat, shuffled his feet atop the ice-covered lake on his way to his fishing hut, which was further out from shore than any other. As he neared Daryl Watson's shack, he lifted a gloved hand and banged on the metal side.

"What you doin' in there, young fella," he said enthusiastically. Daryl pushed open the flimsy door to the hut. He looked tired, his face a bit drawn.

"Hey, Kev..."

Kev is still focusing out on the ice and is not looking at his round friend. He pivoted slowly on the slick surface and faced Daryl.

"Been out here long...whoa, boy, you look like a load of heifers run right over you!"

"Aw, not much sleep last night," Daryl replied slowly, "Julie made some new casserole, I think it had lamb in it. It ain't settling too good." Daryl patted his stomach with his right hand and stepped out of his hut, looking out beyond Kev towards the road. "And I was down in the kitchen last night when the lights flew past."

"Lights?"

"Yeah, a couple of cars. I think one was a cop car, probably county. They was in a hell of a hurry."

"Yeah," Kev said before he asked, "What way were they headed?"

"West." Both men turned and look west, as if they expected to see something of importance. Kev, with over-sized gloves still on his hands, dug at his bushy beard. "Called Will," Daryl continued, "left a message for him when he gets in this morning...you know, to see what happened."

Kev nodded in agreement. He then turned and looked up the lake.

"Yep," he said in agreement then paused, "looks like we had an ice break."

"Where?"

"Up yonder," Kev gestured. Daryl moved around Kev and looked where the glove was pointing.

"Tree branch?"

"Nah, too far out," Kev said before he resumed his slow shuffle on the ice towards the fracture with

Daryl following close behind. Chunks of ice bobbed in the water within the hole.

Kev stopped about ten feet from the hole. Daryl stopped next to him.

"That ain't a break," Daryl uttered, stating the obvious, "that's a hole."

"Yep," Kev replied, urgency in the tone of his voice, "and I think you may wanna go back up to the house and make another call."

35

David Havens, his face red more from anger than the cold, climbed back up the embankment from the lake to the road. Down at the shore, peering into the icy water, was one solitary uniformed officer. Two other deputies milled about the road side and four more lingered by the squad car closest to the County Sheriff as he approached the road.

Wailing sirens grew ever so louder off in the distance.

"Skilling...you and Harper...measure the distance from the road to the fracture," Havens ordered, "and stay off the god damned tire tracks! Curtis, you and Miller shut down this road from both ends, now! No fucking thru-traffic, no fucking exceptions. Go!"

The officers next to the car scattered quickly. Two jumped into vehicles and drove off in opposite directions. Two others, Skilling and Harper, popped open the trunk to one car and began rummaging through it.

"Hey," Havens hollered, "hey, you!"

The deputy at the lake staring at the hole, Smith, realized that the Sheriff was yelling at him.

"Smith...I'm from Towanda...I just came up to fish..."

"Smith...well, Deputy Smith, make yourself fucking useful. Clear everyone off the ice. Get statements from each and every one of them."

"Yes, sir!" Smith started to go out on the ice towards a small contingent of fishermen some one hundred yards away.

"Smith...Smith!" The deputy turned after four steps onto the ice and faced the Sheriff, who was waving at him. Havens face was boiling. "Get the fuck off the ice! Go around...go in over there."

Havens pointed toward the north end of the lake. Smith paused, frozen in fear of the County Sheriff, before he finally scrambled off the ice and hustled through the snow out of sight. Deputy Dunbar, who had been taking pictures with a digital camera, approached Havens. He cautiously pointed at the road.

"There's another set of tracks, sir," Dunbar reported.

"Not one of ours?"

"No, sir, a smaller vehicle."

"Mark it," Havens commanded, "see what you can get..."

An EMT cruiser and a fire truck pulled up near the scene, lights flashing. Another County Sheriff's car whipped up in front of them and stopped in the road. Havens, his rage suddenly raised even more, walked toward the squad car in the road with determined focus. He clenched his hands together tightly into fists as he approached the road. Deputy Brown jumped out of his car.

"Sheriff, there's a body in the yard of a trailer over on Fuller."

Havens spun around and glanced at the lake, where Skilling and Harper were walking. He started gesturing with his hands as he took in the scene here and the news from Brown. There were suddenly more deputies and a few firemen lingering in the area.

Finally, Havens exhaled loudly.

"How long before the divers get here?"

Skilling glanced up at the Sheriff then looked at his watch. "Twenty minutes," he shouted.

Havens looked at his watch and shook his head. Dunbar was now lingering over the mysterious tire tracks on the road.

"Get those pictures back ASAP," the Sheriff yelled, "and I want the make of the other car that was here before lunchtime." He paused and looked at the small crowd gathering down by the lake. "And get me those god damned measurements! Teams of two comb the lake shore in both directions two hundred yards!"

36

Two State Police cars parked at the end of the driveway of the first mobile home on Fuller Road, their strobes lighting up the shining glaze of the snow. Havens pulled his cruiser behind them and left his lights going as he stepped from his ride.

Sirens blared from every direction of the countryside as he stepped into the yard, noticing the large rut in the snow from tire tracks that chunked up faded grass and dirt.

He walked directly at the body face down a few yards from the door, dark flecks of dried blood slightly covered by a thin coating of snow. He stood above the dead man, observing the major wound to the back of its head. He looked again at the spray of blood across the snow, then at the door to the trailer.

"One hell of a collage."

Havens nodded to the State Policeman standing in the doorway.

"Sheriff," he continued. Havens' face dropped. The officer was holding a baby.

"Oh, God," Havens muttered.

"He's sleeping," the Officer continued, "but you're not going to believe this."

Havens took a step and his left foot slipped. He looked down and noticed something under his foot. The Sheriff reached down and picked up a one-hundred-dollar bill that had been hidden under the snow.

"That's nothing," the Officer added. Holding the bill in his hand, Havens walked to the stairs, and stepped past the policeman into the trailer.

"Holy shit."

There were the three bodies in the house, two men and one woman. One man was laid out directly in front of the door and the other man and the woman were at the far end of the living room, close together. The man near the hall was missing most of his head, the remnants of which were scattered on the wall and ceiling behind where the body had been standing. The woman had been gut shot and bled out onto the carpet, which contained a rather large crimson stain. Around the living room were various denominations of bills, some wadded and some perfectly flat. Some were clean; some were tinted with blood.

"Quite the slaughterhouse."

Havens turned to see Stone standing in the kitchen next to the table littered with drugs.

37

Teri, bundled in a heavy coat, rifled through boxes in the attic, sorting some into another box while pitching others into a garbage bag. She came across an old, dust-covered photo album and smiled. The faded blue cover of the large book was starting to peel, but Teri held it as though the cherished item were perfect. She clutched it to her chest for a moment, then grabbed the trash bag and headed down the stairs, letting the attic door slowly close behind her.

As she crossed the dining room to the kitchen, there was a knock at the front door. She paused, as that door is not normally used by visitors – the people who regularly come to the house.

She hurried to the kitchen and dropped the bag next to the back door and the knock resumed.

Grabbing a dishtowel from over the oven door, she wiped her hands as she walked through the house.

"I'm coming," she hollered as she tossed the cloth onto the couch. The knocking stopped.

She opened the door. County Sheriff David Havens stood before her, his hat in hand, flanked by two deputies. All three were stone-faced, solemn.

38

Havens and Teri sat at the dining room table, she had a tissue balled tightly in her right hand and was holding the Sheriff's hand with her left. The other deputies waited stoically by the front door.

"I don't get it," she said through tears.

"We'll find him, Teri," Havens interrupted, trying to comfort her, "that I promise you..."

"No, why was he up by the lake," she questioned. The lawman squeezed her hand.

"That's what I'm going to find out," he said. "Did Will say what he was staking out before he left last night?"

Teri paused for a moment, as though a light had come on. "He said something about drugs in

Catherine, something to do with the car he found in the pines."

"Did he mention Fuller Road at all?"

"No...why? Is that where the drugs are?"

Havens gave her a small, reassuring smile. "No worries, Teri," he replied.

One of the deputies entered the dining room and whispered in Haven's ear. The deputy then leaned back as his boss considered the statement for a moment. Havens nodded and the underling left the room. He then turned and faced the widow.

"I have to go now," Havens spoke with a quiet but powerful presence in his voice, "but I'll be back later. In the meantime, I'm going to leave Deputy Cross here with you. If you need anything, you let him know. Diane is on her way over."

"Your wife is busy, she doesn't have to..."

Havens squeezed her hand again and put his other hand over their clenched hands.

"Will was the best man...he's family," the Sheriff said, "you're family. So, Diane will be here shortly. Do you need us to pick Amy up at school?"

Shock crossed Teri's face as her mouth dropped open and tears began rolling down her cheeks.

"Oh, God, Amy...how do I tell her?"

Havens turned and nodded to Cross, who slipped out of the room and began talking with the other Deputy. "I'm going to have Diane pick her up on the way," he said as he turned his attention back to Teri, "I'll be back as soon as I can."

He slowly withdrew his hands from hers, stood, looked at the weeping woman for a moment, then quietly left the house.

39

Havens arrived back at Ketchler Lake and sat in his SUV for a minute, watching the flurry of activity in front of him. The road was bustling with people; there were a dozen police cars - both County and State Police – as well as fire rescue vehicles, an ambulance, and several private vehicles with blue lights flashing.

He drew in a deep breath, stepped from his ride, and navigated around vehicles until he was close to where Will's car left the road. There were at least two dozen people - cops, fire personnel, and citizens combing the lake shore in a wide swath in both directions from where the car went in the water. Skilling was standing halfway up the embankment, supervising the search. The County Sheriff approached him.

"Nothing on shore, quarter of a mile, either way," Skilling reported, "I'm having the teams swap out and go over the other's side again, just to make sure we didn't miss anything."

Havens stepped carefully over the tire tracks, met up with Skilling, and the two walked slowly down to the water.

"Divers in the water?"

"Been in about five minutes," Skilling answered, "even with thermals, they can only do short stints. Too damn cold."

They stopped at the water's edge.

"Then get more here," Havens barked, "I don't care from where, just get more here. I want a rotation, someone in the water at all times."

Skilling paused as he looked away from the water to the far shoreline, then to his boss.

"Dave, what I told Cross, I'm telling you...he wasn't found in the car." He paused again, as if to find the words. "We did find something, though…"

"What?"

"Money," Skilling replied, his tempo picking up as he spoke, "twenties, fifties, hundreds...in the water. Total so far is a little over 1700."

"Shit," Havens muttered as he looked out over the iced over lake.

"What?"

Havens shifted as he took in this information, then looked at Skilling.

"The shooting up on Fuller. Will must've interrupted a drug deal. That's what he was chasing." He turned and looked at each group walking away from them slowly but steadily in both directions, then shook his head. "Do whatever you have to and get a make on that other car and get an APB out on it. My guess is that car ran Will off the road."

40

The bell rang throughout the halls and the noise din of students talking escalated then faded as they filed into their classrooms.

Amy, clutching a textbook and a notebook, entered room 104. Seated at the teacher's desk in the front of the room was Mr. Curry, the balding 60-year-old Guidance Counselor. He had a stack of papers in front of him.

Just inside the door, first row, second seat, was Becky. Amy and Becky caught each other's gaze for a brief moment.

"Amy, please take a seat on the other side of the room," Curry commanded with a deep voice. Amy continued across the room and sat near the windows. "Now, ladies, this is day one of your detention. You have assignments, I am sure. No talking. Get to work."

Amy glared at Becky for a moment, then realized that Curry was watching her. She looked down at her text book, opened her notebook, and paused.

"Can I borrow a pen? I forgot mine in my locker."

Curry rose from behind the desk and approached her. "It's, 'may I borrow a pen?' And you should always be prepared," he said.

Amy rolled her eyes. "May I borrow a pen?"

Curry chuckled and looked around as if he had made a terrific joke.

"It's the old English teacher in me. Of course, you may borrow a pen." Curry was still chuckling, amused at himself as he walked to his desk, retrieved a pen, and returned to Amy, presenting it in an almost grand fashion.

"Thank you."

"You're quite welcome." He returned to the front of the room and was about to sit when there was a knock at the door. Becky leaned out away from her desk and both she and Amy noticed Glenda, their Principal, peaking in the small window in the wooden door. Curry caught himself in mid-sit, rose, and ambled to the door. The door opened a crack and Glenda's hand waved Curry out into the hallway. Curry stopped before stepping out and turned.

"No talking," he said.

Becky was still trying to see what was happening.

"Who's out there," she asked in a loud whisper. Amy glared at her for a moment then turned her attention back to the door.

"The Principal."

Becky's face dropped.

"Shit. I wonder what she wants?"

"Does it matter?" Amy looked down at the sociology textbook that sat in front of her. Becky had turned in her chair and was looking at Amy.

"I...didn't mean for all that shit to happen the other day."

"Yeah, well..."

"I'm trying...to apologize," Becky pleaded. Amy rolled her eyes again. Becky glanced at the door then back to Amy. "Your dad…is he that tough at home? It's gotta be rough."

"Actually, he's hardly ever there anymore," Amy said as she slammed the textbook closed, "not like when I was younger."

The door opened and Curry stepped just inside the classroom. His face was red and he looked particularly uncomfortable. He looked at Amy, then out the door, the back at Amy once again.

"Amy, would you please come out into the hall for a moment," he spoke quietly, his voice quivered a bit.

Amy sighed and stood. As she crossed the front of the room, Becky looked at her and shrugged. Amy shook her head. Curry stepped aside and Amy moved around him into the hallway. Curry turned glanced at Becky before he closed the door as he followed Amy into the hallway. Glenda stood along the far wall of the hallway, along with Diane Havens. The Sheriff's wife was overdressed in a loud blue, flower-patterned dress.

This, however, was not the thing that caught Amy's eye. Both women had been crying, and Diane had a handful of tissues balled up in her right hand.

"Amy, I need to tell you something," Curry spoke from behind her.

41

At Ketchler Lake, a hydraulic tow-line was rigged to Will's car by a pair of divers. Scooter stood at the back of his rig at the road's edge waiting for the signal to retract his line. One diver emerged from the water and was wrapped in a blanket almost immediately as he climbed the hill. Moments later, the second diver emerged and was met on shore by an EMT with a blanket. The second diver gave a wave and Havens, who was standing next to Scooter, nodded to the mechanic.

Not a sound came from any of the more than two dozen spectators there as the car was pulled from the icy depths, only the sounds of metal scraping on broken ice and water draining from the Taurus.

Scooter wiped tears from his eyes as the car was dragged up the embankment. Once the car was near the road, Havens held up a hand. Scooter stopped the tow. The Sheriff walked to the car window - which was smashed out - and peered in.   There was no body, only a scattering of wet bills that were stuck to the seats and floorboard.

As the afternoon turned into evening, the activity was still high at the lake. Will's car had been loaded onto a flatbed truck and was parked some fifty feet past the point where it left the road. Portable flood lights had been brought in and set up, and the scene still seemed hectic, with police now scouring the area on the embankment and road side.

Havens got into his car and drove past Will's car into the darkness, away from the madness.

42

Teri sat at the dining room table, a cup of coffee in her hands, and a pile of tissue next to it. Her eyes were puffy from crying, although she was not crying now. She was worn down.

Diane, with her blond hair up in a ponytail, entered the dining room from the kitchen. From the living room, Teri's sister, Cindy, quietly joined them.

"Amy's in her room. She's calm now. She fell asleep," Cindy said wearily as she moved to Teri's side and began to rub her sister's shoulder.

"Thank you," Teri replied as she reached up with her left hand and put it over Cindy's. Their eyes met and Cindy tried not to cry as she saw the tears that now streamed down her sister's face. Diane quickly sat next to Teri.

"Maybe you need to lay down, sweetie," she said, concerned, "you need to rest."

"Why," Teri shouted, her face changing from grief to anger in an instant, "why do I need to rest now?" Cindy clenched Teri's hand as her sister went to pull away. Teri turned and glared at her.

"Teri," Cindy spoke calmly. Teri turned back to Diane, who had sat back in her chair.

"No, Cindy," Teri exclaimed before she refocused her attention on the Sheriff's wife, "what good would that do? Will it bring my husband back?"

Diane looked away.

"Teri...stop," Cindy interrupted, "we're just worried about you."

Teri held her gaze on Diane, who was still looking away from the widow, but now had tears rolling down her face. Mrs. Putner watched her for a moment before looking back at her sister. Her face softened, and she wiped tears from her eyes with the tissue ball in her hand.

"You're right. I'm sorry."

Diane slowly turned back to the sisters. "You have nothing to be sorry about. I can't imagine what you're going through."

From the living room, the front door opened. A moment later, Sheriff Havens entered the dining room. He paused and took in the now quiet room, as the women all watched him. Finally, he walked behind his wife, touching her shoulders, before he sat next to her.

"We pulled the car from the lake," he said slowly, "it was empty."

Teri burst out into heavy sobs, and the Sheriff lowered his head. Cindy wrapped both arms around her sister and pulled her tight. After a few moments, Teri pulled away and sat back in her chair, staring at the couple across from her.

"So, what does that mean," Cindy asked, breaking the horrifyingly awkward silence, "does that mean he's alive? He got out and is laying out there somewhere?"

Havens' eyes drift up to Cindy.

"Sheriff, this is my sister, Cindy," Teri said through sobs, "she drove up from Scranton..."

Havens gave Cindy a slight but polite nod.

"...Cindy, this is County Sheriff David Havens. He and Will worked together a long time ago. Went to the academy together, am I right?"

For the first time, Havens showed the weight of the situation. A few tears welled up in his eyes and he looked away quickly without answering. Diane frowned and touched her husband's hand.

"It's okay, David," Teri continued, "you were his one true friend, he always said that." She paused as she watched him struggle to keep it together. "You can cry. You and I both know Will's gone."

43

The quiet of the night has overtaken the Putner home. The house is lit from one end to the other, but the only sounds from within were Cindy doing the dishes in the kitchen, Teri flipping through pages of old photo albums in the dining room, and Amy watching news coverage on the TV in the living room with the volume turned down low.

Teri picked through the albums, pulling random photos with Will in them, and laying them out across the dining room table. She then picked up a piece of paper - the note Will wrote from the night before. She held the it in one hand and a picture in the other. She began to cry as she read the note aloud.

"Teri, it was June 10th at 5:30 p.m. the first time I ever saw you. I remember that moment so many years ago because you were the only light in the dark tunnel that my life had become. I knew I had to meet you, that's why I pulled you over. It's funny how, after all these years, we tend to overlook the good things in our lives for the bad. There is nothing more important in my life than you and Amy, I mean that truly from my soul. Will."

From her left there came an audible moan. Teri looked up and saw Cindy standing in the entranceway to the kitchen, dishtowel in hand, crying.

"That was really sweet," she said. Teri smiled weakly at her sister, and looked back at the picture of her husband. Cindy paused before she continued. "You never told me that you actually met him when he pulled you over? I thought you met at the restaurant?"

"We actually did meet at the restaurant," Teri replied, "but I wasn't his server. He kept asking me for stuff – ketchup, a new fork – and I would send his server over. I think it was Donna."

189

She smiled and Cindy chuckled.

"See? If you'd have brought him the ketchup, he probably wouldn't have pulled you over," Cindy said.

There was a knock at the door. Cindy glanced over her shoulder at the clock in the kitchen. "Who the hell is showing up after ten at night," she wondered loudly. She motioned for Teri to stay, and hustled through the dining room through the living room, passing a zombie-like Amy, who was curled up on the couch.

She opened the door to find Daryl Watson, dressed in camouflage overalls with a dress shirt underneath, and his wife, Julie, standing before her. The shock of seeing Julie's unnaturally dyed red hair with a fluorescent green dress hid the fact that she held something in her hands.

"Is Teri here," Julie asked politely.

"Uh...yeah, she is..."

There was a moment of hesitation by Cindy, and Julie smiled.

"Can we see her?"

"Who is it," Teri hollered from the dining room.

Julie leaned around Cindy. "It's us... Daryl and Julie Watson!"

Teri appeared in the doorway from the living room to the dining room. Amy looked up at them from under her blanket.

"Come in," Cindy said as she opened the door wide and stepped aside. Julie pushed past her in a rush and walked over to Teri, who forced a weak smile as she was handed a dish.

"It's lamb and carrot casserole...my own recipe...it's really good," Julie said quickly but cheerfully. She forced a smile too large for the situation. Daryl lingered behind, a bit uncomfortable. He fidgeted with his hands, his face was red and he did not try to make eye contact with anyone.

"Thank you," Teri said genuinely. Amy stood up abruptly from the couch and went down the hall. A moment later, her bedroom door slammed shut from upstairs.

"Poor girl," Julie sputtered.

"She's devastated," Teri offered. Julie's face went from awkward smile to deep concern then back to awkward smile.

"It's so hard to believe," Julie finally said. There was an uncomfortable momentary pause. Daryl adjusted his feet and quietly cleared his throat.

"I thought something was up last night," he said and everyone looked at him, making him more uncomfortable. He began fidgeting with his hands.

"What are you talking about, Daryl?" Teri asked softly.

"Late last night, a cop car went flying past our place...no lights going but I saw, I was down in the kitchen getting a glass of milk...he was going real fast...I called Will...well, his office..."

Daryl trailed off and he started to cry. Teri slowly walked to him, her face sadness and anguish. She reached up and touched Daryl's round face.

"We are so sorry," Julie interjected, unsure of what was happening.

"It's okay, dear," Teri answered her without taking her eyes off Daryl, whose grief now laid out before her. The large man began sobbing heavily, his body shaking.

"He was my friend," Daryl said as he tried to compose himself, "he always treated me good. He was the best person I ever met."

Teri leaned in and hugged the crying man in her living room, then pulled back suddenly, turned, and crossed the living room to the closet. She grabbed a coat and paced back across the room to the door, crying.

"Thank you for coming," Cindy said swiftly, as she tried to open the door and usher the Watson's out. Teri waves her off.

"No, they're okay," she said as she reached the open door, "I just need some air." She rummaged through her pockets until she brought out her gloves, a few pieces of crumpled paper tumbling to the floor.

Julie glared at her husband, who seemed totally oblivious to the situation.

"Teri," Cindy said.

"I just need to go for a walk," Teri continued. Daryl noticed the papers on the carpet.

"You...dropped somethin'," he stuttered. Teri stopped and bent down, letting out a guttural sigh. She laughed through the tears as she spoke.

"Receipt for chocolate cake in the fridge, which he loves...loved so much, oh and the note I was going to leave for him when I stopped in his office the other day." She held up the note, her hand shaking. "I never left it."

She leaned to the other side of the door and dropped the two pieces of paper into the overflowing trash can. Her incomplete note read, *WILL, I LOVE YOU, CAN YOU...*

On the side facing up, in Will's handwriting, the note read, *2390 Fuller Road $312,000 54 days.*

44

Catherine Baptist Church was a classic old, stone and brick church. It was nestled just off the center of town, only one block from Sheriff Will Putner's office.

The day was bright, there was not a cloud in sight and, for the first time in months, the air was not frigid. Rows of police cars lined the streets around the church and the parking lot was packed full. Inside, the memorial service for Town of Catherine Sheriff Will Putner was going on. The front door to the church opened and County Sheriff David Havens stepped outside. He pulled a cigarette pack from his coat, tapped out a cigarette, and lit it. The church organ blared suddenly inside with a faint chorus of a hymn behind it.

As he smoked, the church door opened behind him, the organ grew louder, and quickly ebbed as the door closed.

He did not turn to see Stone standing behind him.

"Sheriff," the State Police Detective said. Havens exhaled.

"Stone," Havens uttered then paused as he took a drag, "anything new on Fuller?"

Stone rummaged through his pockets and produced a pack of cigarettes. He lit one and leaned back against the brick church wall.

"Believe it or not, it was a meth hub for northern P.A. and southern New York. With 86 right there, they could cover from Jamestown to New York City. They primarily covered Elmira to Binghamton, and down to Scranton/Wilkes Barre. They had quite an area locked up. Even had a tag going up 81 to Syracuse. And they were so far out of the way, no one would give a shit."

"Except for Will," Havens said.

"Yeah, whatever," Stone grumbled, "anyway, the information in that little shithole led us up the chain. A higher up in the pile, a smug little shit named Carver, wanted to know where his product and his money were at. Never mind he was being arrested, going to prison, hell, none of that. He was more concerned about his money, though. Two runs worth. First run was a little off 300k. Second run about 130."

"That's a lot of meth."

"Oh, fuck, they had illegal scripts, H, X, a little of everything. But the meth was his bread and butter...where can I get a good coffee around here?"

"There's a diner one block over on Main."

Stone stomped out the partial cigarette and lit another immediately.

"Yeah, so, that was quite the little piss and fuck they had going on over there."

"So eloquent," Havens snapped.

"I really need a coffee..."

Havens took one last long drag off the cigarette and flicked the butt to the ground.

"So, Will was on to something," Havens said.

"Your boy may have been involved," Stone mentioned.

Havens exhaled and stepped right into larger man's face.

"You fucks ruined his life twenty years ago," Havens hissed with a low growl, "hitting that kid was an accident. IA cleared him, the grand jury cleared him. But you guys just kept riding him, fucking with him. You took away a good cop, made him a shell of what he once was."

Stone smirked.

"Guilt does a lot of things to a man..."

"Yes, it does. And he suffered for it. But that is over with, now. Anything you may be thinking, get rid of it. He's going to be remembered as a hero cop who set off the biggest drug bust in the history of this county, period." Havens then leaned in so that they were nearly touching. "And I'm not going to tell you again."

The smirk left Stone's face. He went to move to his right and Havens mirrored him, blocking him. Stone froze before he spoke.

"Nice memorial for the old boy," Stone finally said.

"Beautiful," Havens replied, "go get your coffee."

Havens took a step back and turned sideways, as if to let Stone pass. With his thick leg, Stone pushed away from the wall and walked toward Main Street.

45

The green Honda pulled into the parking lot of a large shopping plaza and skirted the outside of the lot until it drifted into the darkness around the side of the building. The driver carefully navigated around parked cars and box trucks, then backed into a spot that shielded it from sight between two large trucks.

The driver's side door opened and a man walked around the back of the car, a screwdriver in hand. He deftly removed the OHIO plate from the car and hugged the neatly manicured hedge behind the vehicles until he came to a Mazda parked six spots away. Moments later, he had swapped the OHIO plate for the OKLAHOMA plate, started the car, and pulled back out onto the highway.

As he merged into traffic, he picked the screwdriver from the passenger seat and dropped onto the black duffel bag in the back seat.

46

It was 54 days…54 days from the time David Alan Wallace went off the road and buried his car in the trees to the day good old Daryl Watson found it. I knew it would be found; I counted on it.

I couldn't start a full investigation without it being found; there would have been no reason to. Instead, I would occasionally circle Catherine, looking for anything out of the ordinary.

Back to that night…

I just happened to be off County Road 5 when Wallace blew past me doing 70. He touched his brake lights but when he saw me pull out, he sped off again.

When he went off the road, it was a blaze of snow that looked a mile high…and it was snowing and blowing like crazy. I parked at the road and ran down as best I could to the pines, but when I got there, Wallace was already dead, his head smashed on the window. I still remember taking off my glove, checking for a pulse. He was gone. Beside him, a black duffel full of cash on the passenger seat.

That was the spark.

I stayed there for what felt like forever, but was only ten minutes, waiting...WAITING for someone to drive by, see my lights and stop. But no one did, no one stopped, and fate gave me this option.

The snow had packed and piled tight, so tight that I couldn't get the passenger door shut all the way again. I did what I could and trudged back up to the road, the duffel slung over my shoulder.

I sat in my car for a few minutes still considering all of my options while watching the snow build up quickly. But I would look at the bag with all of that free money, and my mind would wander.

I started the car and left, not seeing another car until I reached town, its headlights snapping me back to reality.

Teri hated my shop, and Amy hardly left her room unless it was to eat, so keeping the money there was a no-brainer. I would go out at night, almost every night, not only to work on my cabinet but to remind myself of the endgame. The money.

When that car was found, it is what I had been wanting for some time. Being able to check the car as a whole would give me an angle, as long as I could keep it in-house. Thank you, Buck.

I knew the State Police would be involved, they try to get into everything. But if I had time, a day or two head start, I knew this would work.

The trailer on Fuller Road...what a clusterfuck! I had counted on everything up to that point but, in the moment, sometimes shit goes sideways. I don't regret killing them…I had planned on doing that anyway. Then dump my car somewhere. Get a jump on everyone.

But going into that lake…fuck! What a stroke of luck that was! I smashed the window out as the car hit the ice and slid out with the duffel and the plastic shopping bag that still had some money in it. My guess is, as that car sank, the police would think I tried to escape but got caught under the ice and floated with the undercurrent down to the lower end of the lake.

It will take weeks – if not months – for them to figure out I'm not there. Hell, they may see this as something never solved…the cop in Ketchler Lake.

When I climbed to shore and made it to the road, the driver of the Honda had been knocked out. He rode with me for a while before he became expendable.

I drove all night, ending up outside of Cleveland, where I swapped out the license plate. After that, it

207

was staying on the main roads, hitting the occasional rest area for food and bathroom, and getting some sleep. I contemplated that first night of going to Canada over Mexico, but two things swayed me. One, money goes a lot further south of the border and, two, I am beginning to hate the fucking cold!

I do feel bad for Teri, and for Amy as well. But the insurance money they will get for my death will more than make up for the loss.

I struggled with this, I really did. There was a moment, the night that ended with chase at Ketchler Lake, where I was ready to back out. But fate presented me this chance.

So, this is it. This clears my conscience.

This is my confession.

Formerly Wilson Putner, Sheriff, Town of Catherine.

47

Will sat in his car, the driver's door open, at the far end of the parking lot of a rest area in El Paso, Texas, with the handwritten note in his left hand. He had written it the night before when he had stopped, and now read it one last time.

He plucked a lighter from the console and touched the flame to the bottom of his confession, letting it burn for a few moments before dropping it to the asphalt. With no one around, he let the embers turn to ash and flutter away in the hot, humid air.

He smiled, swung his legs into the car, and started the engine. His new life in Mexico awaited him.

Made in United States
North Haven, CT
10 March 2023